ART HISTORY

A WOODLAWN COLLEGE ROMANCE
BOOK 1

HARTLEE FINN

BRB BOOKS

 Formatted with Vellum

For Shannon
Thank you for making the space where
Sebastian and Derek were first born.

ACKNOWLEDGMENTS

Art History would have never been finished without the cheerleading of my writing group, Hot Cross Nuns.

It would never have been readable without the unending patience and skill of my editor, Laura.

Y'all made this a great process.

I promise to speed it up next time.

PROLOGUE

THE CRICKETS WERE loudest at twilight, and Sebastian and Brian lay on the hay floor of the fort and listened. One hopped over toward them, sitting just outside the opening to the tarp and chirping happily. Sebastian slowly reached out his hand, and both boys held their breath, but the cricket jumped over his outstretched arm into the ferns nearby.

Brian frowned. "What were you gonna do with it anyway?" he asked the older boy.

Sebastian crawled backwards deeper into the fort. "Show it to you, I guess. You said you lived in the city all your life, so I figured you'd never seen one close up."

Brian smiled. He sat up, crossed his legs, and rummaged in the blue tote bag he always carried. "Oh, I forgot. I brought some gum," he said, pulling out a fresh pack and handing it to Sebastian. The battery-powered light illuminated the fort enough during the daytime when sunlight tended to do most of the work. But as evening crept in, the low white light gave the inside of the fort an eerie appearance. Sebastian situated his fort under the crossing of three downed trees that had succumbed to a summer storm. He's used some old two-by-fours that Manny gave him and created just enough scaffold to use the blue tarp as a sort of tent covering. With the groundskeeper's help, Sebastian had scavenged an old metal table, a wooden chair with no legs, three buckets, and a square piece of corrugated metal that he leaned against one of the trees like a makeshift wall. He hadn't gotten around to finding a poster yet. Manny had said he needed a "pin-up," but he figured that meant a picture of a girl, and Sebastian didn't think that would look right in his fort. Still, he felt like he needed something there.

"I've been thinking about your poster," Brian said, "and I found something, but you can't tell Mr. Shaw."

Sebastian raised his eyebrows. Shaw had all sorts of interesting things in his house, including his own paintings, but he was pretty sure Brian hadn't stuffed one of those in his bag. He watched the boy pull out a National Geographic and shake the pages. A folded map fell out of the magazine. Brian handed it to his friend.

"It's the Bermuda Triangle," he said. "There was a whole article about it. Ships and planes disappear there, and no one knows why." Sebastian smoothed out the map and held it up to the light. Most of the paper was blue, with a dotted red triangle going from the southern tip of Florida over to Puerto Rico and then back up to Bermuda. 'They could have called it the Puerto Rican triangle, too,' he thought, turning the map this way and that.

"It's so weird, but I thought you could hang it on the wall, and we could plan to go there one day. I bet if we study hard, we could solve the mystery and find out what happened to all those people."

Sebastian held the map to the wall. It was just small enough to fit. He held it in place and helplessly looked for something to adhere it with when Brian pulled closer with a roll of cellophane tape. He stuck the bottom two corners and then leaned close to attach the two corners Sebastian held up. He looked closely at his friend and, for the first time, noticed how his blond hair had streaks of gold woven in it. Brian should have smelled just like Sebastian since they used the same soap. But his own scent was a bit like the woods, all pine needles and bark. Brian, Sebastian thought, smelled like sunlight.

"There," Brian said, leaning back. "We can work on this together. My mom always says it's good to have a project." He handed the magazine over. "Read that. It's really weird. I bet Mr. Shaw has other books we can look at."

Sebastian smiled and started paging through the magazine. "So, we're gonna solve the mystery of the Bermuda Triangle?"

"Yes," the boy said, leaning out to see how far the sun had set. He suddenly pulled back and raised his index finger into the sky. "It's a date with destiny!"

They both burst out laughing.

SEBASTIAN TATE DUCKED as another pile of paper rained down onto his head. The tower of journal articles and student papers had been teetering for months, but in his haste to grab a book of Picasso prints, the entire bunch shifted, showering him in scholarship. He stood behind his desk looking at the mess, the Picasso book dropped at his feet, and wondered how the undergraduate essay now sticking out of his coffee would change its taste. Would it be bitter? He pictured this semester's students in his art history class. Surely.

"Dr. Tate?" a voice called from just outside the door. He could see the shadow of Angela, the department secretary, on the other side of the frosted glass. Sebastian sighed and counted to three. A gentle knocking only just preceded the woman pushing her way in. "Oh, what's happened here?"

He held up his arms in an attempt to explain and immediately gave up. "Me, that's what happened." He sat down in the hard-wooden chair with a thump that made his teeth rattle. "Is the semester over yet?"

"Have you turned in your grades?"

Sebastian looked at his briefcase, stuffed with the rest of the undergraduate essays. "No," he said.

"Well then, it's not over for you, is it?" She moved a stack of overdue library books and sat across from him in a much more comfortable, padded chair. "I have a few registration forms for you to sign for your advisees, and I want to remind you about the meeting."

Sebastian reached down for the Picasso and laid it on his desk, his reason for retrieving it long forgotten. "Sure. I thought we were signing digitally now. I just got the hang of it."

"They're switching systems right now because fall registration is the best time to install a new system." She smiled the sarcastic smile that usually confused Sebastian.

"What meeting?"

"The new president is meeting with the department today for a luncheon. Eleven sharp in the O'Neil Room."

Sebastian sighed. The O'Neil was a new conference room on the other side of campus. The idea of trudging across the sunlit campus full of fresh undergraduates playing Frisbee and not doing work filled him with a sudden dread. He tried to make himself smaller in his office chair in the hopes of disappearing.

"Why are you personally escorting me to this meeting?"

Angela smiled. "You're the only one I think won't show. So, up," she said, rising to her feet. "Let's go."

<hr>

SEBASTIAN KEPT his head down and pretended to look at his phone during the walk across the campus quad. He made noncommittal motions with his fingers on the screen, trying to mimic what he'd remembered students often doing in his class. His cousin, Denise, bought him the smart phone for Christmas last year, and as of today, it hadn't been charged up for a week. He simply forgot, and the only one who called him on the phone was Denise. As they neared the new building that contained the O'Neil Room, Sebastian thought he'd have to plug it in when he returned to his office, so at the very least, he could listen to his Denise's annoyed messages.

The rest of the College of Arts and Science were as already present—at least those Sebastian knew. Having delivered her package successfully, Angela made her way to the front of the hall, sitting herself by the provost...Anderson or Andrews? Sebastian wasn't sure. He forgot what a provost was and turned away. He'd spied the coffee table as he entered and made his way there, scouting for an empty seat in the back. A familiar voice called to him, and he sighed with relief.

"Here, Tate. I saved a spot." Dr. Mark Willoughby pointed to an empty chair next to him. The plump engineering professor sat before a small pile of pastries recently plundered from the buffet table. Today he wore a bright orange Hawaiian shirt and cargo shorts. As he approached this unlikely friend, Sebastian thought, this man carries the sun within him every day of the year. Willoughby passed the art professor a croissant and leaned close. "Didn't think Angela was going to let you escape this one. I hope you tried at least."

"I'd forgotten about the meeting, so I forgot to hide."

"Ah, well. Maybe this time it's for the best. How often do we get a new president?"

A balding man sitting in front of the two men turned around. "I can't say I'm happy with the way this selection went about. We, on the search committee, were not even consulted."

"Well," said Willoughby, "I heard there was a lot of money

added to the endowment. Perhaps that trumps the search committee now."

The man sniffed. "I expect the two of you to co-sign a letter from the college about this indignity. I will email it later today." He spun back in his chair as the Dean took to the podium. Willoughby looked at Sebastian and rolled his eyes.

Disinterested in the administrative ceremonies of academia, Sebastian sipped his coffee and scanned the room, taking inventory of who may have successfully escaped this torture and promising himself to be scornful of them later. Near the front, one figure caught his eye. A new face, he thought. It couldn't be the new president, not that young.

The man sat a little off to the right of the stage, watching the Dean make his opening statement. He had wavy hair, reddish nearing blond, but closely shaved on the bottom— what the students called an undercut. He seemed relaxed in the way a lounging predator is relaxed, tightly wound and ready to spring. He sensed danger coming from this man, not physically, but existentially. Sebastian looked at his fellow faculty and wondered why only he seemed anxious.

The people around him were politely clapping, and Sebastian realized the Dean had finished his speech and the young man leapt from his chair to the podium. "Thank you for that wonderful introduction, and I apologize for taking the faculty's time away at such a busy time of the semester. I promise to be brief." His voice was baritone, not deep, but with threats of going deeper, and he spoke with a smooth quickness that made Sebastian catch his breath. This man he'd never seen before, never met, felt too familiar, and all of a sudden, Sebastian wanted to flee from the room and lock himself in his office. He was staring at his smile as the man talked but wasn't paying attention to what he was saying until Willoughby said, "oh shit" and leaned back in his chair—the rest of his bagel uneaten. Sebastian turned to him, desperate to break away from that face and those—surely, he couldn't tell from back here—green eyes.

"What? What did I miss?"

"Open your ears, man. He's cutting the College of Arts and Science faculty by 30%. I don't even know if he can do that."

By the time Willoughby had said the word "cutting," the rest of the assembly erupted with the realization that some of them would not be returning next fall. Sebastian stood up and looked for the exit. Willoughby called after him, "Don't worry, Seb. You've got tenure," but Sebastian needed to leave as the remaining faculty got louder and louder. That voice and those eyes. Why had it affected him so much? How did he know this man? He burst into the sunshine and found it a welcome relief. He needed to get back to his office and his papers and his books and the familiar smell in the dust of all the professors before him. He needed to bury himself in those final papers and desperately try to forget.

2

NOT LONG AFTER the meeting had started, the quad had emptied of students, most heading back to their dorms to pack for the summer break, the rest burying themselves in the library to study for their last exam. Sebastian headed straight for the art building across the grassy square, thankful that he didn't have to pay attention to Frisbees and laughing coeds. Head down, he plunged forward, not wanting to look back, only to move ahead into the safety of his office. He exited the field and started down the cobblestone path, shrouded by old elms. The glare of the sun couldn't penetrate the shade here, and he often read here; it was his favorite spot for reading once the students had gone and before the full humidity of the summer rolled in. Sebastian pushed his hands deep into his pockets. He clutched his office key so hard he could feel every nook in the metal.

The wave of fear and—something else—washed over him back in the O'Neil room so fast that he hadn't had a chance to register the bad news. Surely, he would be safe from the staff cuts, he thought. He'd been tenured five years ago and had consistent, if not enthusiastic, student evaluations. He practically was a one-man art history department. The new president guy isn't making that drastic of a change, is he?

The phone in his pocket kept vibrating, adding to his annoyance. He stopped in the shade of an elm angrily, punched the button, and his cousin's voice cut through the air. "Finally! I've been trying to get you all week."

"I can't talk right now, Denise. Can I call you back?" He hunched down, keeping his back to the quad and acting like a conspirator.

"You won't. I'll call you tonight." There was a muffled conversation in the background. "You answer. Don't make me come up there."

He hung up without saying goodbye, confident that if he didn't answer his cousin's call that evening, she'd be on the next train from Washington, D.C. The last thing he wanted was guests, though, granted, he had the room. In just a couple of weeks, Woodlawn College would be quiet for the summer. He neared the end of the path, thinking 'Just a few more weeks and a few more steps.'

Sebastian stopped just outside the main entrance to his building. The young president's face flashed in his mind, and this time, those eyes were looking straight at Sebastian. He sensed them on his back as he left the room, but the feeling dissolved in the sunlight. Now, in the gloom of the deserted entrance way, he felt those eyes upon him again.

"It's Dr. Tate, right?"

Eyes wide, Sebastian pulled his keys out of his pocket, wielded them like a weapon, and spun around. "What are you?" he said, his right hand held before him.

The new president stood about ten feet away near the edge of the sidewalk, half in the sun, half in the shade. His hair was aflame with the sunlight, but everything under his eyes was in shadow. Sebastian suspected he smiled. "My name is Derek Morton. The meeting just ended, but I noticed you left early." He took a few steps toward Sebastian, who instinctively took one step back. "I didn't want there to be a misunderstanding."

Sebastian lowered his arm. "What would I have misunderstood? You've come to cut faculty. I may be one of those let go."

Derek said nothing and kept smiling.

"Am I?" Sebastian repeated.

"That hasn't been decided yet. And it won't be decided by just me if you think this is a shake-down."

Sebastian tried to stifle a giggle and failed. "Shake down. I haven't heard that term in forever." He coughed and looked back at the new president. Handsome, tall, so cliché. Yet, at the moment Sebastian laughed, he'd noticed a small flinch in his otherwise confident demeanor. The professor relaxed a bit.

"Well, if you want me to make my case, then come to my office, but don't think I'll enjoy it." Sebastian flung open the ornate oak doors of the arts building entrance, one of the oldest structures on campus. The offices were coveted by everyone who didn't spend a summer wrestling with the persistent wasps that took up residence in the house there. He heard the doors close behind him and wondered what other kind of pest he just let in.

3

THE PROFESSOR unlocked his office door and motioned that Derek should enter. The frosted glass had a slight crack along one of its edges, and the lettering making up the words "Art Department" had started to peel in places. Derek peered into the gloom before Sebastian turned on the lights. He said, "I don't get many visitors, and I normally meet with students in the atrium."

He motioned to the only chair not filled with printouts and folders. The room was on the larger side, but Sebastian had added additional bookshelves sticking out perpendicular to the built-in units. It created a used-bookshop vibe that seemed particularly in line with his demeanor. Derek peered at some of the shelves before sitting down in the ancient leather chair. Green shades covered two-thirds of the windows that looked out onto the quad. What little sunlight entered the office had to fight with the elms before reaching Sebastian's desk. In lieu of this, he turned on a green desk lamp better suited for a Victorian clerk's desk than a 21st-century professor's. Derek chuckled, feeling like he'd leapt back in time twenty years. "The office seems to suit you," he said.

"Does it? Well, I suppose offices do that after a while." Sebastian looked up from his desk. "You say that as if you know me."

"This is a rather large office, wouldn't you say?" Derek dodged smoothly. "For such a young professor, that is."

Sebastian seemed to tense. "I'm not that young, and this office was bequeathed to me by its previous occupant." He shifted in his chair and rolled the pen on his desk. "Besides, no one wants to deal with the wasps."

"Wasps?" Derek asked, looking around the room as if one would swoop in on cue.

"Never mind that. What do you want to talk about?" Sebastian sounded as if he was holding back his frustration, only a little.

Derek looked around at the stacks of books and boxes. He pointed to something in the far corner. "Those canvases back there. Are they your work or the work of students?"

"Canvases?" Sebastian asked, his forehead wrinkled in confusion. "Ah, those. They were also of the previous occupant." Derek watched his face, searching for some clue as to Sebastian's feelings about the paintings or the previous occupant. The man just deepened his slouch and mumbled. "They are not much for..."

"Shall we take a look?" Derek bolted out of his chair and grabbed the first canvas from the stack. It was a small oil painting of the entrance to the university. The bronze letters of the Woodlawn College crest were speckled in the shadow of the large oak tree near the front gate.

"This is a nice one," Derek said. "Though I don't know much about art, I think I would like this for my office."

Sebastian looked at the man and then down at the painting. "You want to take it?"

"It's just sitting in a pile here anyway, right?" Derek asked.

"Right, but..." Sebastian trailed off, looking at the rest of the pile where a thick film of dust sat accusingly along each side.

"Are there more like this?" Derek said but made no move to rummage through the rest. He watched the professor closely to gauge his reaction. When he'd visited the campus during his interview, the legacy of Campbell Shaw had been downplayed by the dean of business. The trustees talked excitedly about events at Shaw Manor and the paintings the landscape artist left in the school's custody. Sebastian rubbed the back of his neck, obviously growing more uncomfortable by the minute. Derek wondered if he should push a bit more. His phone alarm sounded, and looking at the screen, he swore under his breath.

"Sorry, I'll have to continue at another time. I've got to meet with the deans." He closed the gap between him and Sebastian, getting closer but just far enough to be businesslike. This time, Sebastian didn't retreat.

"I'm going to take this one with me. I would love it if you could pick out a few more of your friend's pieces for my office." He smiled at the small painting in his hand. "This style suits me, like your office suits you." Derek smiled and walked past Sebastian toward the door.

"How about tomorrow afternoon, around 3? I can send someone by to grab the canvases before then, and we can decide together where to hang them up."

"Yes?" Sebastian said.

"Great! It's a date. A date with destiny!" Derek said and pointed to the ceiling. Sebastian stared back at him, the look of confusion still firmly planted on his face. The man chuckled, then left the room.

———————

THE DOOR CLOSED WITH A THUNK, but not before Sebastian heard, "Tomorrow then," echoing in the hall outside.

"A date with destiny," he repeated to himself. It was an odd, childish thing to say. What destiny had brought this man to his college and his office? At that moment, it certainly felt more like a curse.

Sebastian made his way back to his desk, sat down hard, and leaned back in his chair. The phrase was so weird, but something familiar tickled his mind. He looked at the leaning row of canvases and scowled. He'd go through them tomorrow morning. The guy evidently didn't care what Sebastian picked, so why put more effort into it? He rubbed the back of his neck again. Since moving into the office, he'd never once looked at those paintings. It had been too painful at the time and, after so many years, too weighty of a task. Twelve, no, now eleven paintings by his mentor and guardian, and he'd just let them lay in the corner, collecting dust.

Perhaps it was time to let them go. It annoyed him that it was this new president that made him finally take notice of them. Maybe the misery associated with them would go as well. He closed his eyes and listened to the buzzing of the approaching summer. 'Damn wasps,' he thought.

4
———

SEBASTIAN, 7 years old

Campbell Shaw inherited the house from his grandparents, he told Sebastian's mother. He would never have afforded this on his professor's salary, and if there hadn't been an endowment plus help from the historical society, he'd never been able to keep up the place, let alone live there. Beverly, his housekeeper, and Manny and Jim, his groundskeepers, were all paid for out of the endowment to keep the manor in the family and out of the public domain.

"The partnership with the historical society is helpful too. Through grants, we can do a lot more with the gardens and open them up for free to cultural events and concerts. Next year, we're thinking of doing a hedge labyrinth—though I doubt Manny is looking forward to that."

Sebastian watched his mother laugh, and it calmed him. That laugh and his father's strange giggle were the two sounds in the world that assured him that everything was good and safe. He felt strange being in this big house with this new person, but his mother said he was a friend of his father. So that meant he was a friend of Sebastian's as well.

"Since Harold will be here and since this place is huge, it seemed only right for you both to tag along. There are plenty of empty rooms for you to choose from. There's a nice one off the kitchen that gets a lot of light but little noise. That might make a good office for you," he smiled at Sebastian's mother. She was a writer when she wasn't a teacher. "Thank you. I'll take a look after tea."

"And you," he said, ruffling Sebastian's hair. "You can have the run of the place as long as you listen to not just your parents but Beverly and Manny and Jim. They're the bosses of you from now on."

"Yes, sir," Sebastian pouted but was secretly ecstatic. Who knew what kind of treasure and ghosts and mysteries an old mansion like this held? He promised himself to examine every door, every panel, and every bookcase that could be hiding a secret entrance. If Sebastian had his way, he would take apart this old house, brick by brick, just to see if there was a ghost inside.

Sebastian found Manny right away. He was leaning over a particularly prickly hedge and swearing. The sudden appearance of a child startled the big man, and he gave a little yelp when Sebastian's face appeared.

"You must be Harold's young man," he said, taking off his glove. He held out a well-worn hand for shaking. "My name is Manfred. You can call me Manny. What may I call you?"

Sebastian, all of seven years old, looked up at the man with his mouth agape. He'd never been addressed as an adult, and he wanted to make sure he didn't mess it up. He squared his shoulders, put his feet together, and stiffened like a robot. He shot out his puny arm and let it disappear into Manny's.

"My name is Sebastian Tate," he shouted, trying to sound older. "And you may call me Sebastian, Mr. Manny."

The groundskeeper gave a couple of hearty pumps to the tiny hand and laughed. "Just Manny is fine. I hear you're going to be around this summer. That true?"

Still excited by his new surroundings, he answered. "Yes. My father is studying under Mr. Campbell, and my mother will be writing. I am," he paused as if remembering something important, "to stay out of trouble to the best of my ability." The boy grinned.

"Ah," Manny said, nodding. "To the best of your ability, eh? Well, that's the loophole in the contract. See, perhaps you're old enough for adventures, but not too old to understand your ability. Right?"

Sebastian stared into Manny's sweaty, pink face. He felt like he was being let in on a secret. He also felt like he was getting his very first accomplice. Although he didn't have a name for it yet. In the end, Sebastian was making his very first friend.

"I like adventures," was the best reply he could muster.

His new friend laughed even harder. "I bet you do, Mr. Sebastian. I bet you do." He squatted down at eye level in front of the boy and confided in him.

"I'll send you on your first quest, shall I? My assistant, his name is Jimmy, is supposed to be clearing out some brush at the edge of the forest down this path. Do you see where I'm pointing?"

Sebastian looked past the prickly bush to a well-worn footpath in the wildflowers. He could see about fifty feet before it curved off.

"Now, I have a feeling he's taking a nap. I don't blame him. We get really busy before the summer months, so he's been working hard. But I want to make sure he gets in here for lunch, otherwise, a Hungry Jimmy is a Cranky Jimmy. You know what I mean, right?"

Sebastian nodded, wanting to understand the full stakes of his job.

"So, for your first task, I need you to follow that path until you come to the edge of the woods. Don't go any further. If you see Jim, wake him up and bring him back. If not, just come back right away. You understand?"

Sebastian nodded again, hopping from foot to foot and eager to get moving. He wanted to walk through the wildflowers, see the edge of the forest, and wake the mysterious Jim.

"Now wait. Are you allergic to bees?"

"No."

"Poison Ivy?"

"Nope."

"Any other allergies?"

"Nuh-uh." The boy was hopping up and down now, warming up for a track meet. Manny laughed again and wished he had half the energy.

"Ok. Go!"

Sebastian took off down the path—half running, half skipping—wanting to complete his quest but also wanting to see where the path led. After the turn, there was a brief incline as if the garden behind him lay in an indentation in the surrounding field. As he drew nearer the forest hedge, he realized that most of the property was bound by this shallow forest, and he thought about treehouses, forts, and hideouts. He wondered if Manny would help him build them.

Deep in his daydreams, he didn't notice the man before him, and he walked straight into the backside of Jim. The man turned and growled. Blood covered his face and shirt. He smelled of copper and sweat.

Sebastian bounced back and fell on his rump. He looked up into the face of horror and screamed. He held his arm over his face and screamed and screamed, and a moment later, he was lifted into the air. Two strong hands held him aloft and moved him forward, back down the path toward the house and Manny. He choked a breath and screamed again, and the hands under his arms gripped tighter, and the pace quickened. As soon as they turned the corner, Sebastian saw Manny running toward them, having heard his screams. His face went from worry to whimsy when he saw what approached him.

"Mr. Maaaaaaaannny!" Sebastian sobbed and held his arms out to be transferred to his new and only friend. Manny dropped to his knee and took the boy in his arms. He patted him on the back and let him calm down. Sebastian heard him say, "What the hell is all over you?"

"I didn't touch him until he started screaming. Then I brought him to you! I don't know where he came from. I…ugh…this is all a sticky mess."

Sebastian stifled a few tears and braved a look at the man he'd run into. He made sure to stay well within the safe grasp of Manny.

"It was that damn raspberry jam that Donna made for me." Jimmy tried wiping all the red goo from his face but only succeeded in smearing it some more. Sebastian could smell the sickly sweetness coming off him, and his terror subsided. "I was prying the jar off when it BLAM," he waved his hands around his face and chest, "just exploded all over." He kept trying to clean himself and kept failing. Manny suppressed a laugh and also failed.

"Ha ha," Jimmy said, "wasn't funny when the wasps came. I just fought one off when the little one showed up and ran into my backside."

Manny fell back onto the ground and started roaring. How Sebastian's screams had terrified him. How he ran as fast as he could to get the boy. He'd only met him this morning, and he was being as protective of him as his own sons. Wiping tears from his eyes, he looked at Sebastian, whose own tears were drying on his confused face. "Mr. Sebastian, please say hello to Jim. I promise he will make your summer here very interesting."

Jimmy stuck out a raspberry jam-stained hand and then pulled it back. "Pleased to meet you, Seb. I better go get the hose."

In Sebastian Tate's seventh summer, he received his first two friends, his first nickname, and the fright of his life. He sat on the ground with Manny and smiled.

5
____

SEBASTIAN SIPPED the cappuccino the engineering professor had just brought him. The pastry-eating man watched from the guest chair as Sebastian sat on the floor and pulled out the canvases. Some art students had left a respirator mask behind at some point and he was damn glad he found it. Each canvas he pulled from the stack brought a new shower of dust and dirt. He wished he'd thought of removing his sweater and working in his T-shirt. Too late for that now.

"Should have brought one of those portable vacuums," Willoughby said from behind him. "When was the last time those pictures were moved?"

"They've been here since before my time. They were Shaw's paintings. I didn't feel right moving them, I guess."

"Ah, dear Shaw. He was a true Woodlawn man. Are they all landscapes from around campus?"

The four that Sebastian had removed had all been scenic views from the different corners of campus. Two had been set in the winter, one that looked like mid-summer, and this last one was fall and looked to have been painted looking out one of the office windows. Sebastian never took much to painting himself, spending more time in discovering the hidden meanings in images, the subtle discourse of sculpture, the way an entire generation could speak through art. He envied the practical art professor; those usually elbow deep in ceramic or oils. As he carefully flipped from one canvas to another, he felt unsure of his importance. Perhaps his specialty was just as a hanger-on, not producing anything but confusion and resentment in undergrads forced to take his class as an elective. Impostor syndrome was a constant companion in Sebastian's life, but since Derek's arrival, it seemed unnecessarily present.

Willoughby looked over his shoulder at this last one. "You can really see how much the elms outside have grown. Also, how much better things are when you actually open your blinds all the way?" Sebastian turned his head and scowled at the man. "Can't be all emo all the time, Seb. Gets lonely."

"Not as long as you're around," Sebastian answered.

"Why'd you decide to go through these paintings today, after all this time?"

Sebastian wasn't sure why he kept Derek's meeting and request a secret. Partly, he suspected that Derek, with his cost-cutting strategy, as it was being branded, was the enemy, and he didn't want to be seen as a traitor. That wasn't the whole story. Derek Morton affected him in ways that were still occluded by memory. There was a familiarity to his attitude that Sebastian didn't understand, and something about his manner pulled him forward, like a fish on a hook. Sebastian needed to understand the connection before explaining it to anyone else, even Willoughby.

"Procrastinating from final grading, I suppose," Sebastian finally answered. "Plus, this corner could be the source of my wasp problem."

Willoughby jumped from the chair. "Right. Forgot about that. Well, I'm off. Enjoy your paintings and your coffee and your stinging friends."

Sebastian smiled and reached for another canvas, this one quite larger than the rest. After blowing off most of the dust, he noticed that an oil cloth covered the face of this canvas. Moving the smaller pieces aside, he carefully set the painting down on the floor in front of him and lifted the oil cloth. Sebastian gasped and kicked out at the painting, pushing it as far away from himself as he could.

"What is that doing here," he thought, and he felt a sudden urge to light the thing on fire, and possibly to light the whole world aflame.

6
_____

Casey Stanfield didn't expect his summer fellowship to turn out this way. The title "Executive Research Assistant" sounded elite, and it drew a lot of applications from the College of Business. So, he was surprised that he landed the role. He was pretty farsighted for a twenty-year-old and took every opportunity that came his way to make the most of his time at Woodlawn. When he saw the notice for this summer fellowship, he jumped on it, even if his chances were slim. Now, standing outside the arts building and pulling a hand truck behind him, Casey was questioning his life choices. At least the office is on the first floor, he thought.

He'd barely rapped on the frosted glass when the door swung open, and a haggard man with longish black hair motioned him in. His arms and shoulders were covered in a layer of dust, and his eyes were red and watery.

"Dr. Tate?"

"Yes, yes. You're from Morton? They're right there." The man pointed to a stack of paintings leaning against an overladen bookcase. He turned away from Casey and stood at the back of the office, looking out the window. "There are five paintings there. You shouldn't need my help, right? Don't worry about being careful."

Casey weaved the hand truck around boxes and other detritus on the floor. "Mind if I move some of this out of the way?" he asked to the professor's back.

Sebastian turned abruptly. "Oh, I'm sorry. Let me..."

Casey held up a gloved hand. "It's fine. I can do it quickly. I'm on lacrosse, so this is easy." He hefted two heavy boxes and moved them to an open spot near the desk. Wary of the stacks of loose paper, he gently shifted things enough to move freely. "Besides," he said, grunting a bit when moving the box of books, "you look like you're having an allergy attack."

Dr. Tate blinked and touched his face. "Yes, allergies. It must be all the dust." He smiled, but just at the lips, and turned back to the window. "Do you know where those go?"

Casey gently set down the last box. "Yup, President Morton's new office, I think. It's nice of you to donate these." He started carefully placing each painting down, separating each canvas with the cardboard sheets he had been given for the job. It felt strange to talk to the professor's back, and he hoped he wasn't annoying. He hadn't spent much time in the arts building. His curiosity was piqued by the somber tone of Dr. Tate and the cavalier attitude of the new president. Casey liked people, and he especially liked that they came in all stripes.

"Oh," he said, taking a moment to look at one of the paintings. "I like this one."

Dr. Tate seemed to stiffen but didn't respond.

"It's the one that looks out that window," he added, feeling the need to explain.

The professor relaxed and turned. "Ah, that is a nice one. The campus shines in the fall. My mentor and my predecessor in this office painted that. He left them here when he... well, they'll have a much better home on the wall in the president's office, I think."

Casey paid little attention to the rest of the canvases, much more interested in the art professor's unease. The man reminded Casey of another student he'd seen around campus, another person who made him curious. He strapped a bungee cord around the bundle on the hand truck and wheeled the package back through the maze on the floor. "This is all of it, right, professor?"

The professor returned to his watch at the window. "That's it. Take them."

Casey nodded and left the office. As he wheeled the bundle across the quad toward the administration building, the sunlight caught the edge of a brass frame poking out of one of the wrapped canvases. This one had shown the front of a brick house but at a weird angle. He didn't understand much about perspective but thought you could at least put a person in the painting. Art was for people anyway, he thought. Casey sighed, knowing he'd be spending the beautiful afternoon inside hanging old landscapes. He pushed on, momentarily distracted by a group of young women sunbathing at the edge of the quad, the brick house forgotten.

7

"YOUNG PRESIDENTS ARE NOT unusual at small colleges like ours," the Dean of Business was saying. The man was secure in the knowledge that Woodlawn's Board of Trustees had made a fine choice in the new president, one with a focus on vocational training instead of the usual philosophical adherents to a bygone era. Derek Morton held only an MBA from the State College of Pennsylvania, and that, along with his youth, made him a bit of a unicorn in collegiate circles. However, he had presented a bold plan to the board—a way to save money, reinvest in the student body, and "catalyze the university as a 21st-century institution."

'Did I really say that?' Derek thought, watching the Dean's animated face talk about distance learning and practical curriculum and blah blah blah. He smiled and glanced over the man's shoulder. Casey should be back soon with his paintings and, more importantly, an anecdote of his meeting with Sebastian. All day, the president had wanted to wander the campus, take in the sites like those in the paintings, and maybe just happen upon the art department offices again.

But all day, he ended up sitting in his too large office listening to the blathering of one administrator after another. Soon, there would be a break and a chance to hang up some pictures before being monopolized by the Dean of Student Affairs.

"How many Deans do we have on this campus?" Derek asked, at first not realizing he'd said it out loud. Seeing the Dean of Business taken aback was worth a lean-in. "Could you send me the latest organizational chart of the entire administration when you get back to your office?"

"The whole thing? I'm not sure I even have a…"

"Surely this is right up the College of Business's alley, right? Who else could I trust to give me important insight into the organization of the college? Business or non-profit, it doesn't matter. A hierarchy must be maintained. Can you help me with this?"

That's how you get buy in, Derek thought, using another phrase he hated. "Buy-in" makes everything transactional. In his more cynical moments, he understood that for many people, everything was transactional.

"Yes, I'd be happy to help," the Dean of Business replied.

Derek heard the sound of metal wheels on tile out in the hallway. "Thank you. I look forward to working closely with you on a number of matters here at Woodlawn." He held out his arm to indicate the meeting was over, and the Dean, half flattered, half flustered, left the room, nearly colliding with Casey, who waited just outside the door.

"I like this fall scene, Dr. Morton. You should put this one on the wall across from your desk." Derek studied the piece closely. The painting showed the view from Shaw's old office window. If he took Casey's suggestion, he'd have a simulacrum of the view Sebastian had now. There was something in the kid's suggestion. "Yeah, go ahead and put that one there. It's not doctor, by the way. Derek is fine."

Derek grabbed the next painting in the stack. This one was not a campus scene but something from the surrounding countryside. Woodlawn College was situated in the middle of farming country, and this painting reminded him of Andrew Wyeth's famous piece without the young woman in the field. "This could be from any number of places outside of campus," Derek said.

Casey struggled to see as he held the fall scene to the wall, marking spots for the hangar. "Mr. Morton, shouldn't maintenance be here to do this? I mean, what if I mess it up?"

Derek looked up from the painting. "Yeah. Go ahead and fill out a request for me. I don't have the hang of the ticket system yet."

"Sure," said Casey, climbing down from the table and settling on the office's small sofa. He opened his laptop to start the request.

"What was Dr. Tate like when you went there?" asked Derek. Then, thinking the question might sound suspicious, he added, "Was he annoyed?"

"The professor? Nah. He had everything ready for me, so I wasn't there long." He tapped on his keyboard, paying more attention to the form than Derek's question. "There was a lot of dust. I don't think anyone's looked at these paintings in years."

"Ah, yes, I noticed that." Derek had a million small questions he wanted to ask but didn't think the new president would dignify himself by acting like a lovesick kid. His new assistant didn't seem to notice, but Casey seemed more perceptive than the average undergrad.

Casey leaned in toward his screen. "He seemed upset, too.

He said it was just allergies from the dust, but I got the impression he'd been crying." He slapped his laptop closed and looked directly at Derek, extinguishing any idea that he was only slightly paying attention. "I'm not sure, though. He was definitely tense. And I'd bet money that someone tried to burn that big painting in the past." He pointed to the large canvas still covered in oilcloth.

"I don't think it was the professor because of all the dust, and I got the feeling he wanted all of these paintings out of his office as soon as possible." Casey stood up, packed his laptop into his backpack, and slung it over his shoulder. He started for the door and looked back. "You two have a history, don't you?" he asked.

Derek smirked at his boldness. "Why do you say that?"

Casey shrugged. "Just a hunch. Maintenance should be here on Tuesday. Bye." He left the office at four p.m. on the dot, leaving Derek with the uncomfortable realization that he wasn't able to maintain the cool exterior he'd cultivated. 'At least, not about him,' he thought, walking over to the large painting. His fingers slid over the oil cloth, and he tugged playfully at its edges.

"I wonder," he said to the empty office.

8

SEBASTIAN, 10 years old

Sebastian sat on the wooden seat and swung his legs back and forth. Manny had been pushing him back and forth, but when the station wagon arrived, he had to take care of the family. The swinging slowed, and the boy's attitude dropped with each motion. He hung his head. Mr. Shaw said that he would teach him how to paint, but all he'd been doing was drawing in an old book. Now, with the guests arriving, the boy felt like the man would have no time for him anymore.

The swing stopped, and Sebastian slowly turned in a semi-circle. The breeze spun him so he was facing the driveway. Shaw was hugging a young woman who stood by the wagon. They smiled at each other, and Sebastian felt a strange twinge in his chest. She opened the back door, and a young boy, close to his own age, hopped out onto the gravel. He hugged his mother's legs, looking up at the older man who greeted him. Sebastian watched the boy closely. He looked shy and small.

Shaw waved for Manny and then pointed toward the elm. As Sebastian watched, the groundskeeper approached and called his name. "There's someone Mr. Shaw wants you to meet." Sebastian hopped alongside the tall man and stopped just beyond the group. Shaw leaned down and stretched out his hand.

"Come closer, Sebastian, this is Brian." The small boy hid behind the woman's legs, staring. Sebastian took a step forward and said, "Hi," as quietly as he could muster. Normally the only child hanging around the estate, he felt, in the presence of such shyness, he should tone himself down. The boy just watched him.

"Brian is a couple of years younger than you, Sebastian, but I hope you can be friends while he and his mother visit."

Sebastian nodded, beaming at the responsibility he'd been given. "Do you want to see the fort I've built near the garden?"

The boy's eyes widened. "A fort?"

"Yup."

"You built it?"

Sebastian puffed out his chest. "Yup. Wanna see it or not?"

The boy looked up at the woman. They had matching blonde hair, matching blue eyes, and matching smiles. "Go along. Manfred will keep an eye out for you?"

"Yes, ma'am," he said, piling the luggage near the steps to the large manor house.

Sebastian held out his hand, "Come on. I'll show you, and, if you're tough enough, you can be a member."

Brian took the hand and held it tight. "I want to be a member of the fort," he said, laughing as he was being pulled along.

SEBASTIAN BLINKED in the morning glare. He unstuck the side of his face from his desk and cringed at the large drool puddle he'd created overnight. He hadn't fallen asleep in his office in years, and even then, it was usually only at the beginning of the semester when he was frazzled and disorganized. He hadn't drunk so much either. Rummaging through those dusty paintings had left Sebastian with a strong thirst and a desire to forget. After a short drive to the liquor store, he found himself turning back to campus, hiding in his dark office, and watching the light fade through the elms. If he'd been caught getting drunk in the arts building, he'd probably be fired. 'That's probably going to happen anyway,' he thought, and quickly downed a glass of water on his desk.

Unfortunately, it was gin.

He spit out the foul liquid into his garbage can and slid off his chair onto the floor, completing the look of the drunk professor. I'll live on this floor now, he thought. He lay his arm over his eyes and sighed. The forthcoming depressive episode was going to be a doozy. He could feel it. At least the campus was quiet. It was the Saturday after finals. Most of the students and faculty had gone for the summer, and the only stragglers were those who still had to turn in their grades.

Sebastian scurried across the floor like a crab and fumbled for the papers in his backpack. He pulled out two stacks of term papers and, with dread, turned to the back of the first one. He slumped, sighing with relief. He hadn't been sure, but after checking each one, he appeared to have graded everything already. He crawled back to his desk and pulled his laptop onto the floor with him. Slowly, he started inputting the grades into the college's system. The spring semester was officially over for Sebastian, and the burgeoning hangover suddenly split his head in two. He closed his eyes again and waited for the pain to pass.

He tried summoning the dream again, the sunshine childhood he remembered at the manor. As he drifted into a dense nap, his hand twitched, still feeling the small warmth of Brian's hand in his. Sebastian's fingers searched for the threads of his past, clasping at nothing.

9

SEBASTIAN, 10 years old

The summer storms kept the boys inside all day, and after three summers of investigation, the manor house had relinquished all its secrets to Sebastian. Now, he could experience every corner of the building anew with his friend at his heels. He and Brian climbed the pull-down staircase to the attic and sat under the circular window. The dull light that poured in did little to illuminate the surrounding room, but they had been up here so many times that they could navigate it blindfolded. They sat there, listening to the drips from the small holes in the roof, and waited for the excitement. Sebastian looked up from his book, some pulp thriller he found in Shaw's office, and glanced over at Brian, who shivered a bit in the damp attic. He wasn't small for his age, but frail, and in comparison to the ever-growing Sebastian, he seemed much more than two years younger. He sat cross-legged on a pillow, thoroughly engrossed in another issue of National Geographic. Sebastian leaned toward him and saw pictures of dolphins and those other ones, the black and white ones.

"They're orcas," Brian said. Sebastian started and saw he was being watched. "You looked confused, and I figured you knew what a dolphin was. These," he pointed to the full picture of the orca, "are mammals too. They're pretty cool but a bit scary."

Sebastian leaned back. "Yeah. How many of those have you read this summer?" He touched the corner of the magazine.

"Hmm, a lot. I haven't really kept track."

"But you could go online and learn all that stuff." Brian nodded. "Yeah, but this is different. Like, I would have to already know what I wanted to read. In this," he held up the magazine, "they put a bunch of stuff together, and I don't have to choose."

Sebastian nodded at Brian's obvious genius and went back to his thriller. The assassin was searching for some woman in a warehouse, and he was bored, bored, bored. He dropped the book again and leaned back, his hands behind him in the dust. The window shimmered with a flash of light. Sebastian waited.

The thunder peel shook the house. It started with a low rumble and, like a whip, crack shot out like a cannon of the gods. Sebastian gave a little "whoop" when he heard it, and he suddenly noticed a new but familiar smell in the room. Cowering above a spreading puddle, his magazine tossed aside, Brian was violently shaking. He clutched his thighs to his chest and buried his face in his knees. Sebastian asked, "Are you okay?"

"Don't look at me!"

Sebastian put his hand on the boy's back, surprised and scared at Brian's reaction.

"Are you hurt? What happened?"

He could hear the boy sniffling. "The lightning. The storm. I hate them." He looked up, and Sebastian's heart sank. Tears streamed down the boy's face, his expression full of misery and shame. "I get so scared. Please don't look."

Sebastian got up and grabbed an old blanket from one of the boxes. He pulled a couple of pillowcases, too. "Brian. It's okay. That thunderclap scared me, too."

Brian's sobs only got stronger. "But you didn't pee your pants." The last few words cut off in a wail.

Sebastian knelt. "That's only because I'm more used to them than you. After a summer here, you won't be scared ever again."

"You sure?"

"I promise." He ruffled the blond hair on his friend's head. "Now, stand up. Go over there and get undressed. You can wrap yourself in this blanket. Put your clothes in this pillowcase, and we'll explain to Beverly."

"No," Brian said, taking the blanket. "I don't want them to know."

"It's fine, it's fine. Beverly keeps all the secrets. Just get changed."

With his wet clothes in a pillowcase and another set of sheets absorbing the puddle, the two boys descended the ladder and found Beverly in one of the upstairs bedrooms, vacuuming. The look on her face when she saw these two would make Sebastian giggle at the memory for years. The older boy quickly explained the situation. She smiled and ushered Brian into the bathroom to get him sorted out.

"You go downstairs and get some lunch, I'll send him down after you," Beverly said, shutting the bathroom door.

On his way to the kitchen, Sebastian decided to peek into Shaw's office to look for another book, something with more action and fewer women. 'Women always slowed the story down,' he thought, sliding the office door open, 'so boring.'

The door stopped on its latch, only allowing an inch or so of opening. He realized Shaw must be painting and didn't want to be disturbed. He peeked, hoping to get a look at his canvas, but his setup was out of view. Between the gray light of the stormy afternoon and the yellow warmth of the fire stood Brian's mother, naked and holding a small bouquet of primroses at her side. She was looking perpendicular to the door, most likely to where Shaw was sitting. Sebastian was awestruck. His eyes were drawn to the yellow and lime sweater she always wore, crumpled on the floor. He felt shame and curiosity, but the overwhelming feeling was concern. He was sure that Brian didn't know his mother was in here, showing herself like this to Shaw. He didn't think his friend, who couldn't handle one thunderstorm, could handle this confusing scene. He looked again at Brian's mother, at her body. It made him angry, and he didn't know why. He quietly slid the door shut and ran to the kitchen.

Sebastian spent the rest of the day in silence, and Brian blamed himself. He thought Sebastian didn't want some crybaby who wets his pants as a friend anymore. He followed him around like normal but didn't try to make the older boy talk. He didn't want to give him a chance to make fun of him. 'That's not like him,' he thought. If Sebastian didn't want him as a friend anymore, Brian understood. He tried to stay brave all evening, even as the wind picked up and a new round of thunder approached. If his mother noticed a change in the boys, she never showed it. All through dinner, she and Mr. Shaw just chatted and laughed, only occasionally noticing their presence. Brian climbed the stairs behind Sebastian as if he were heading to his own funeral. When they reached the top, the first crackle of thunder sounded in the distance. Brian gasped.

Sebastian turned on him. In the dim light, Brian couldn't see his face, but he'd been waiting for this moment and prepared himself to take the news like an adult. He balled his small hands into fists at his side, but Sebastian grabbed his right arm and pulled him forward.

"You can sleep in my room tonight. I think the storm is going to be bad. You won't be scared if you're with me." The matter-of-fact way that Sebastian spoke made Brian realize his shame was misplaced. He silently followed his friend into his bedroom. "Do you need anything from your room?" Sebastian asked.

"No," Brian said, his voice squeaking. "No. And thank you. You sure you aren't mad?"

Sebastian stopped pulling the covers down and spun around. "Mad? Why? What? Why would I be mad?"

Brian's eyes started to well up, but he forced himself not to cry. "I just- you were so quiet all night. I thought," and the tears let loose, "you didn't want to be my friend anymore."

Sebastian rocked his head back and sighed. "Ah, no. That's got nothing to do with you. I, well, my stomach was a little upset. That's all." He moved to the other side of the bed. "Get in."

Brian jumped on his side of the mattress in awe that Sebastian had a bed much bigger than his twin. "I wanted bunk beds, but Shaw said there weren't any in storage. But there's plenty of room for you."

Thunder rolled again, and the two boys tucked themselves in, deciding to leave the lamp light on in case they had to get up. Sebastian lay on his back and said, "You're my best friend, Brian. What kind of friend would I be if I let you go because you're scared?"

He turned to face him. "That's when being a friend matters most."

Brian watched his friend's eyes flutter and then shut, wondering what other burdens were pushing him to sleep. For a long time, he just watched Sebastian silently, watching each breath as if it was him once more saying "best friend." Lightning lit up the world, and Brian shivered, but for the first time, he wished the storm would never pass.

10

HE WONDERED ABOUT THE DREAM, more invention than memory. The meeting had been real, but the manor house was far grander in the dream than in reality. The gravel driveway had never been that wide, certainly nothing large enough to fit a station wagon sideways. Manny wasn't one to greet visitors, as few as there were. His main role was taming the gardens and doing renovations in the manor. He remembered the boy, though, Brian. Sebastian opened his eyes and traced the faded water stains on the tiles. Where was he now, he thought?

'Ah,' he remembered. 'He's gone.'

The sun fought against the thick cloud cover, foreshadowing a humid Pennsylvania summer. What light made it into the art department office had little energizing effect on Sebastian. He stayed prone on the floor, staring at the ceiling, working through a disorganized stack of memories. Forty-five minutes later, when Sebastian had nearly convinced himself to return to an upright position, someone knocked.

'The semester is over,' he thought. "No," he said to the ceiling.

"Dr. Tate? I saw your car outside. It's me, Casey." There was a pause. "From yesterday?" Another pause. "I took those paintings away?"

Sebastian closed his eyes and strained all his core muscles to sit up. "Errrug, yes. Casey. Hold on." It took him several tries to get on his feet, and in the end, he had to climb up the back of his office chair while hoping it didn't roll away from him. He wiped his face with the back of his hand, glad that he thought to lock his office door before becoming blackout drunk the night before. He was two steps away from the door when it opened, Casey hesitantly sticking his head through the opening.

"Ah," Sebastian said.

"Dr. Tate, sorry. It was taking you a while, and I was worried. Can I come...wow!"

"What, what is it?" Sebastian said, panicking.

"You look like total shit. Are you sick?" He retracted his head a bit as if to ward off some exotic virus. "Should I call someone?"

"Is it that bad?" He looked around for a reflective surface and then thought better of it. "It's just a hangover, Casey. What do you want?"

Casey narrowed his eyes and then nodded. "Oh, I smell it now. Bad night?" he whispered and softly entered the room.

Sebastian wondered at this sudden casual tone they were experiencing, particularly since he only met Casey yesterday. "Uh, is there something I can do for you?"

Casey smiled. "Yes, actually. And I'm only asking like this because I saw your car while I was on my morning run and thought I'd stop by. There's no real urgency to this."

Sebastian got the impression that under all that casualness, there was indeed a sense of urgency, but his mind was too cloudy to care. "What is it?"

"You're teaching Retrospectives in Modern Art in the fall, right?"

Sebastian looked confused. He rubbed his face and combed back his black fringe with his fingers. "Yes. You're a business major, right? That's a higher-level art history course."

"Business for now, and I know registration is over, but I wondered if you could let me add it."

Sebastian leaned away from the kid. He settled back into his office chair and fumbled through one of the many piles of paper on his desk. Students marveled at the ease at which Dr. Tate could find anything. Sebastian knew that it was mainly luck. "Ah, here," he said, handing the printout to Casey. "I knew I put prerequisites in the course description. You've taken these two art history classes?"

Without hesitation, Casey answered, "Nope."

"You need them for the class."

"Okay. Can you teach me over the summer?"

"What?"

Casey straightened up in the chair and placed his hands on his knees. Determination and professionalism washed over his face, and Sebastian would have been impressed by the change had his brain not been swimming in pain and regret.

The kid gave him his pitch. "Would you be willing to work with me over the summer so that I have the necessary knowledge to take your Retrospectives in Modernism class in the fall?"

Sebastian looked at the empty glass, so recently filled with gin, and wondered if his hangover was just an extension of his drunkenness. "I don't understand what you're saying."

"You don't have to formally teach me. Maybe just give me

the syllabus for each class, and I can do the reading on my own. I'd even be willing to take each final exam to prove that I can handle the class in the fall."

The hangover was taking a toll on Sebastian's attention span, and as the sunlight warmed up his already stuffy office, the pain was slowly transforming into nausea. This kid's sudden interest in art perplexed him, and he wondered if somehow this involved a girl. The thought annoyed him. "Look, Casey. As you can see, I'm not in great shape at the moment." He pulled more papers from a completely different stack. "If I give you my syllabi, would you promise to get the hell out of here?"

"Absolutely," Casey whispered excitedly. Smiling brightly, he took the two handouts from Sebastian and looked at them with great eagerness.

"Come talk to me later this summer about the exams and the class. I can't make decisions right now."

Casey jumped to his feet and headed for the door. "Wait," Sebastian called to him. "I'd appreciate it if you could keep my current condition between the two of us. I assure you this is not typical."

"No problem, professor. I won't tell a soul. Not even the new president." With a wink and a smile, Casey turned and got the hell out of Sebastian's office.

Sebastian stared at the door agape, and before he could wonder what the kid meant by that, he made it just in time to throw up into his garbage can.

11

THE FIRST WEEK after the end of the semester was reserved for department meetings: wrap-ups and debriefings, what went right and what went wrong, etc. In Sebastian's experience, they were nothing more than bitch sessions that allowed faculty to air the grievances they'd been holding back all semester. He could see their usefulness, but he could also see their senselessness. Most of the staff just wanted to get away from campus for a bit. The old brick buildings, the quaint garden footpaths and bridges over the stream, the tree-lined quad and verdant green lawns were enough to drive anyone mad in their yearning for the city. As one of the oldest and smallest liberal arts colleges on the east coast, Woodlawn had a reputation as a stepping-stone to prestigious graduate programs and corporate executive rooms. The grounds were beautiful, wild in places and tailored in others. The academic atmosphere was inclusive and accommodating. The faculty-to-student ratio was small and allowed students to work closely with their mentors. Woodlawn was the embodiment of liberal arts education, and by the end of the spring semester, Sebastian hated the place.

Willoughby had a knack of finding him in any meeting room, no matter how far into the background Sebastian attempted to disappear. "I'm kind of excited to come to the meeting this time," he said, pulling up a folding chair next to the frowning art professor. "This one should be a real barn burner."

Sebastian sighed and gave his friend a side-ways glance. "Why does an engineering professor get to come to our meetings?"

Willoughby laughed, bouncing the neon coconuts on his Hawaiian shirt—the only kind of shirt he wore. The rumor was that he owned hundreds. They had been teaching in nearby rooms all semester, and Sebastian tried to keep track. When he counted the twentieth variety of pineapple shirts, he gave up. Willoughby wasn't a collector but a connoisseur. "I teach two science and literature classes, you know, that gives me a free pass into the star chamber." He flexed his hands out and spread them wide as if showing off the room to a potential buyer.

Sebastian sniffed. "Good, then can I go to the College of Engineering meeting instead? I doubt the physicists get into a rhetorical debate about the wording on the agenda."

Willoughby laughed. "No, but there have been fistfights over the snack table."

The last few faculty members settled into the room, followed by the Dean of Arts and Sciences and the new president. Sebastian sank a bit lower in his seat, hoping not to catch Derek's eye, but he failed immediately. Derek raised his hand to wave at the professor and said, "Thanks for last week." Sebastian nodded, trying to ignore the looks from his colleagues, and cursed Derek for being vague on purpose. Willoughby leaned over and said, "Should I ask?"

Sebastian shook his head. "It's nothing. I gave him those old paintings I had lying around for his office. That's all."

Willoughby looked surprised. "I don't see how getting cozy with the new president is going to do you any favors. He's not exactly popular outside of administration."

Sebastian shrugged, trying to keep his head low while keeping one eye on Derek. The man worked the front of the meeting room, shaking hands and giving concerned nods to the faculty sitting up front. The row consisted mostly of new hires and those with an agenda item, and Derek spoke with each in turn, never dropping his salesman smile. Sebastian scowled and turned toward his friend.

Willoughby was watching him with interest. "Paintings? Not the Shaw landscapes?"

"What of it?" Sebastian asked. "They were collecting dust." He folded his arms over his chest and tried to make himself even smaller. "They were a fire hazard," he added.

"Right," Willoughby said, leaning back. "Not the hundreds of books and paper stacks. No, the paintings, they were the hazard. I never thought you'd part with anything that belonged to Shaw." The engineer smiled, and Sebastian caught the implied remark.

Before he could reply, the dean coughed, and the two professors blushed, realizing they were being scolded. "Sorry," they both whispered.

AFTER A BRIEF RE-INTRODUCTION by the dean, Derek stood up and addressed the group. He'd been working on this presentation for the last two weeks, and it was only yesterday that he had the grand idea to play it by ear. The choices were made. There were a lot of discussions and spreadsheets that justified them, but no one in this room would be interested in that. They just needed to hear whether they would have jobs come fall. Derek explained, clearly and concisely, that most of them would, a few of them wouldn't, and one or two were balancing in between.

He found Sebastian the moment he entered the room and waved, but then tried very hard not to look his way. Derek worried that his true feelings would show through, the second guessing and the regret. Part of him knew he couldn't keep that hidden from Sebastian. Under no circumstances could anyone think that he had a soft spot for the professor, especially not Sebastian himself. So, when the man stood up and said, "What the hell is a probationary period?", and the Dean asked him to save that for a separate meeting, and Sebastian described in detail where and how that meeting should take place—"when hell freezes over"–Derek finally built up the courage to look Sebastian in the eye.

"It took a lot of effort to not eliminate the art department all at once. It's not an application department outside of Dr. Fennel's drawing classes. A need has to be shown for these art history classes, especially the upper-level ones."

"We have students in the program that..." Sebastian asserted.

"You have seven students, two of whom just graduated."

Sebastian fumed, and Derek wished that this conversation could take place back in his own office. "The need for art history?" Sebastian said, as if this could be questioned.

"Or the desire, whichever you like. The fact is that those classes don't fill, and filling classes is what funds the college." The faculty started murmuring, and the word endowment was tossed around by the more securely employed. Derek kept his eyes on Sebastian, who hadn't yet sat down. He stood there, his black hair disheveled and coming out of his short ponytail. Derek thought the blue shirt and black jeans were the same ones he had worn a few days ago. Ever since he'd visited his office, the professor seemed off-kilter. Casey's assessment loomed in the new president's head as well. Sebastian appeared to be searching for his words when the teacher sitting next to him pulled on his sleeve. The two looked at each other, and Sebastian slumped and then sat back down.

Derek felt the back of his neck get hot as he wondered who the other man was and how close the two of them were. "Mr. Morton," the Dean was saying, "do you want to schedule the next meeting?"

Derek took a deep breath. "I am under no delusion that there will be a next meeting like this. I fully expect the College of Arts and Sciences faculty to meet on their own and discuss how they can save the jobs of their colleagues. I assure you that without some miracle, they cannot, but I will not dissuade them from finding a creative solution or preparing new demands for the university. In the meantime, I would like to schedule a meeting with the two professors on probation, and I will make myself fully available all summer for any other questions." He clasped his hands together and muttered, "Thank you," and left the meeting room. The dean, realizing his abandonment, quickly followed him out the door. Once the door closed, the volume in the room doubled.

12
____

Willoughby waited for Sebastian to say something first. His own classes had been spared, and for the most part, he was shielded by the College of Engineering, of which he was also a member. He tried to think of something funny to break the tension but decided not to. In the past few days, he'd watched Sebastian go into the deepest depressive cycle he'd ever witnessed. Normally, there would be dips at the beginning and end of the semester when the workload was at its peak. Willoughby could usually motivate the professor out of his funk with a few well-timed coffees and jokes. This time was different. This time, Sebastian was just sad, plain, old, wet down to the bottom of your socks, sad. He looked at the man sitting next to him and wanted to cry with him. But Sebastian wasn't crying. He just sat there and stared. Willoughby wanted a coffee, a donut, and an escape route.

THERE WILL BE NO DAMN individual meeting, Sebastian thought. The last thing he wanted to do was be alone in a room with Derek Morton. Since his introduction meeting, the man had had a strange effect on him, as if there was some unfinished business with this man he'd never met. His aversion contained a mix of confusion and fear, and every time he saw him, Sebastian worried that some long-forgotten memory would resurface and change everything. Not since Shaw Campbell had his disposition had he been so tied to another person.

He stood with his back against his office door and tried to avoid a panic attack. Someone knocked. He screamed.

"Dr. Tate, are you okay?" called Angela from the other side.

Grasping his chest, he willed his heart to stay in his chest. He moved away from the door to the guest chair near his desk. "No, yes, either way."

The secretary entered and took in the situation quickly. Nothing seemed out of place. The normal debris of academia was strewn about the room. Sebastian was sitting in the wrong chair, but it was the look of terror on his face that caused her to drop her backpack and kneel by his side. "What the hell has happened to you?"

"I got some bad news at the meeting, and I'm just not handling it well, I guess."

She nodded. Her instinct was to take his hand and try to calm him down like she would one of her sons, but Angela's professionalism kept her at a proper distance, and she rose and got the professor a glass of water instead. She held it out to his shaking hand. "It's not just about the announcement, is it?"

Sebastian stopped before taking the water, his arm stretched out. He looked up at her, and tears started streaming down his cheeks. He was just as surprised as she.

"Dammit all," she said and put the glass down, taking both

of Sebastian's hands in her own. "I don't know if you can tell me what's happened, but I'll be damned if I won't try to help." She held both his hands between her own and watched him. The tears turned into a full sob, and after a few moments, as he calmed down and caught his breath, he unleashed everything that he thought would explain what was happening to him.

"Nothing makes sense, but somewhere," he said, "it makes total sense."

Angela didn't express confusion or concern or say a word. She sat there with her hands covering his and listened.

13

BRIAN, 8 years old

Brian had never had a better summer than when he and Sebastian ruled the grounds. The manor house and Shaw's staff couldn't hold the two boys inside every day. Even on rainy days, they'd be off, chasing each other through the gardens, swimming in the nearby stream, building, dismantling, and rebuilding forts in the nearby forests. Outside was the whole world, and they felt instinctively a part of it. Brian still needed to be coaxed into an adventure or two, but his admiration for Sebastian eclipsed most of his fear. He followed the older boy everywhere.

"Now this place," Sebastian whispered, "is haunted. One of the gardeners told me that we have to stay away. He said there may be treasure in there, but he's sure there's a dead body." Brian gasped at the idea of a dead person so close to them. He looked past Sebastian into the dark opening of the cave. The ground cover gave way to ribbons of granite, and an old stream carved its way into the rock in this part of the woods. Only a rivulet of water ran into the cave now, but the speed at which the water moved suggested that once you went in, you would be heading downward into the depths. Brian looked back at Sebastian. His friend looked frustrated.

"I know I'm not strong enough yet, but I'm going down there one day. I need to see what's in there." He looked at the ground and kicked at a dead branch. "I need to."

Brian felt so small and so helpless in the face of his friend's frustration. "When you do, I will go with you," he said. "I want to help."

Sebastian looked into Brian's eager face and clapped a hand on his shoulder. "Nah, you'll still be too little even then. Don't worry. I'll bring back the treasure for you." The boy stood with his hands on his hips, the epitome of the young hero. Brian's stomach flipped, and he hoped this summer would never, ever end.

THE NEXT MORNING, a sharp peel of thunder startled Sebastian out of a dead sleep, and he ran to his bedroom window. It was still dark, and morning didn't seem to be on the horizon. He watched the lightning and rain for a while, marveling at how deeply the trees could bend without breaking. He turned back to face his bed and, in a flash of lightning, saw that at some point, Brian had crawled in with him. The younger boy was sound asleep. Sebastian looked back at the storm whipping against the window and decided to climb back in bed. He patted Brian on the head, turned away, and fell quickly into a deep sleep.

When he woke later, he was alone and assumed that Brian

had already headed down to get breakfast. Sebastian had just pulled on a pair of torn jeans when Brian's mother opened the door and asked, "Is my son here?" Sebastian turned and, in embarrassment, covered himself, though he was mostly dressed. He dropped the pretense when he saw the look on her face.

"He was here last night. I think the storm scared him. But I just woke up, and he was gone."

She moved toward Sebastian, her eyes filling with anger. "What have you done with him?" she asked, grabbing his shoulder. Sebastian was tall for his age, but the woman still had a foot on him, and her grip was painful. "Where is he? He follows you everywhere!"

Tears started to fill Sebastian's eyes, partly from the pain of her grip but mostly from a fear building inside him. He needed to see Brian right now. He had an overwhelming desire to see that his friend was safe. Shaw burst into the room and grabbed Brian's mother. He pulled her close and said, "Everyone is looking for him, Jenny. Don't worry. It's a big house, and he could just be wandering." Shaw's voice was soothing and confident. Over the shaking shoulder of Brian's mother, he looked down at Sebastian, who was still crying. "Seb, finish getting dressed and meet up with Manny. You can show him some of the places you two go, okay?"

Sebastian sniffed and stood to attention. "Yes, yes." He finished dressing and took the stairs two or three at a time. He found the groundskeeper outside sitting in the golf cart he used to inspect the property. "Get in, buddy. We're doing search and rescue today!" Always a big fan of the cart, Sebastian jumped into the seat next to the big man, but his empty stomach seemed to roll as guilt and worry started to take the place of excitement. The two headed off to the western stretch of the property, near the tree line and the small forest Sebastian and Brian called their "Adventure Zone."

"You two usually play around here, right?" asked Manny. He wore a bright red windbreaker and a Yankees cap. He slowed the cart to a natural opening in the trees. A path that Sebastian and Brian had worked on all summer to keep clear lay between two great oaks. Sebastian tried to jump out of the cart, but Manny grabbed the back of his shirt. "Oh no, not alone. Give me a second." He switched on his walkie-talkie.

"Hey, this is Manny over by the western tree line. Seb and I are going into the woods to look around and see if the boy went in there. I'm leaving the cart outside so you can find the path if you need to send someone in, okay?"

The voice of Shaw, staticky but clear, came back. "Thanks, Manny. You keep an eye on Seb, he'll get away from you if you give him the chance."

Manny raised a burly red eyebrow at the boy, who hung his head at the same time he hopped in place, ready to bolt. Manny pushed the talk button and held the walkie-talkie to the young boy's face. The groundskeeper nodded.

"I promise not to run off, Mr. Shaw."

There was a pause, then a click. "Good. Go on now." And with that, the two searchers walked into the forest, the rain-water collected by the canopy dripping on their worried brows.

It was one of Manny's men who found the tracks. Working through the woods parallel to them, they heard a shout coming from their left and then a voice on the walkie-talkie. "Boss, looks like someone with small feet came through here not too long ago. I'll shout out so you can find me. There's a second path."

Sebastian heard the second shout and tried to picture where the other man was. He froze. Manny said, "What is it?" Wanting to waste no time, the boy grabbed Manny's sleeve and said, "I know where he is. There's a shortcut to that path over here." Manny said nothing but followed the fast boy as closely as he could.

Sebastian ducked and bobbed as someone who'd traveled the path hundreds of times with Manny struggling to keep up. They ran into Manny's helper, Jim, who was squatting on the ground, staring into the mud. He looked up.

"It was just a hunch. When I saw some broken branches over there, I came this way," he explained, standing up to point out the area. "Then I came across a large spot where it looked like someone fell. There was an indentation in the mud; though, it could have been a deer that decided to stop in the rain."

Sebastian listened and shifted his weight from foot to foot. Manny noticed the boy looking past Jim, down the path toward the granite outcrop. Manny held up a hand to the man, who stopped talking.

"Where did you two go?" he said, bending down to look Sebastian in the eyes.

"We didn't go in," he shrieked and started to cry. "I told him we can't. I told him. He can't have."

Manny grabbed Jimmy, and the two men raced to the opening of the cave. The rivulet was a small stream now, the rain swelling the large creek, and the water needed a place to go. When Sebastian ran up behind them, he saw a blue bag leaning against a small pile of granite stones. The tote bag was Brian's. It held his snacks, leaves and rocks he found interesting, and his adventure notebook. The two men called down into the darkness. Sebastian fell to his knees and grabbed the bag. He curled his arms around it, desperate to keep it clean, to keep it dry, to keep it safe.

As Manny shouted orders into the walkie-talkie and Jimmy attempted to shine his flashlight as far into the cave as he could, Sebastian sat in the mud and cried.

14

"I DON'T REMEMBER MUCH of the next few days," Sebastian said. Angela handed him a cup of tea and slid a wooden chair close. He'd been talking for over an hour and felt like a burden. Yet, Angela hadn't asked one question or made one comment. She allowed him to take a break while she made tea. He saw the face of someone willing just to listen. Sebastian took a deep breath and continued.

"I'd been staying at Shaw's since the accident. My father's family was still fighting over who would take me in. I was happy there. I could pretend it was any other summer when we'd all been there as a family. Brian's showing up had made even the dark moments shine. He treated me like a hero, and ultimately I betrayed him."

"They had to pull me away from the cave entrance when the fire department arrived. I remember Beverly taking me to the bathtub and washing off all the mud. I remember lying in bed, still clutching that blue bag of his. Beverly brought food, but I don't think I ate much. I just knew that Brian hadn't come back. A day or two later, I came back from the bathroom, and someone had taken the bag. I searched frantically for it, screaming and crying. Beverly and Shaw came running in, but by then, I was inconsolable. It was the only thing I had, and it was gone. A doctor came, and then there was a lot of time lost."

Angela took the empty teacup from Sebastian and waited. "His mother, Brian's mother, showed up in my room one day. I couldn't look at her. She just stood there." He started to tremble. Angela placed the cup on the floor and grabbed his hands again. "She stood there for the longest time, and then suddenly, she ran to me and hugged me. I didn't understand. I just cried. I thought she'd forgiven me for leading her little boy to the cave." Tears streamed from his eyes, and his shaking grew more violent.

"She whispered in my ear. 'It's your fault I've lost my boy. You took my light, and I hope you will always live in the dark.'" Sebastian broke into sobs and slid off his chair, Angela moving with him. She hugged him while he cried the tears of a boy.

Sebastian's office faded as the afternoon wore on. Angela turned on the overhead lights and noticed the leftover canvases on the floor. Sebastian, much calmer now, gathered some books to take home in the hope of staying clear of campus for a while. Angela invited him to dinner, but he declined. He wanted to sleep in his own bed and imagine a world outside of Woodlawn. "You've been clearing out?" she asked, pointing to the paintings.

"Ah, no. Someone requested a few of the pictures, and I obliged. They're not... They don't hold good memories for me, anyway." He slung his bag over his shoulder and patted his pockets, making sure he had all he needed. The desk phone rang. Sebastian and Angela looked at each other. In the last ten years, he could count on one hand how many phone calls he received, let alone on the landline. He answered, "Hello?"

"Dr. Tate. It's Derek Morton."

Sebastian stiffened but tried to betray nothing to Angela. "Yes, Mr. Morton. Is there something you need? I was just heading out."

"I was hoping we could talk. Are you free this evening?"

Sebastian sighed. "I think I need a few days to think about this situation. I've only gotten the news today, and I'd appreciate-"

"I don't want to talk about your job, Sebastian. I want to talk about one of the paintings you sent me."

Instinctively, Sebastian knew what painting he meant. He could see the red brick facade of the manor house, the cement planters lined up under the windows, the gravel driveway creeping in from the bottom. He thought he heard the crunch of tiny sneakers running toward him.

"Please, Sebastian. If you could come to my house tonight, we can talk over dinner."

Sebastian held the phone as if he had forgotten how to use it. He looked at Angela for a moment and then, thinking he'd asked too much of her already, covered the receiver and said, "You go on. I'm fine." He waited until she closed the door behind her before replying, "Look. I'll play this out, but I don't know what you're after."

There was a soft chuckle on the other end of the line. "Sebastian, I promise you. It will be alright. Just come."

He gave up. If this Morton guy wanted to torture him, well, he'd have to get in line behind the extended queue of his demons. "Fine. What's your address? I can leave now."

Silence.

"Morton? Where do you live?"

"Dr. Tate," he finally answered. "I'm the president of the university. I live in the President's House. I believe you can see it out your east window."

Sebastian bent down and looked out the far window in his office. In the distance, he saw a man waving at him. "Ah," he said. "I'll be right there."

"Try not to get lost on the way." Derek laughed and ended the call.

15

DEREK MET him at the door, wearing jeans and a T-shirt. He could smell something meaty and delicious coming from the kitchen, and his stomach gurgled at the aroma of barbecue. "I hope you like pork," Derek said, leading him into the kitchen. "I've been marinating this all day and-"

"I'm a vegetarian," Sebastian said. His mouth watered as he got closer to the stove. He had no idea why he lied. His instinctive mistrust of this man made him want to keep the real Sebastian hidden.

"Ah, that's too bad. I can make you a salad to go with the asparagus I was steaming." Sebastian smiled and nodded. He hated asparagus, yet now he was committed. He pulled out a chair from the modest kitchen table and set down his bag.

"Where's the painting?"

Derek looked up from the cutting board. "Can we eat first? You look hungry."

"In all honesty, I don't want to be here."

"But I'm the president, so it's hard to refuse me, right?"

"I guess."

Derek smiled, left the half-chopped vegetables on the counter, and sat down across from Sebastian. "I'll have to keep that in mind. So, why did you pick that painting for me?" He pointed past Sebastian's left shoulder. Sebastian turned to see the manor house landscape leaning against the wall. It was a large canvas, three feet by two feet, with a lot of red and green. Shaw had worked on that piece in the last year of his life and sealed it with a tinted shellac that gave the entire image a sepia tone. He'd never understood that choice; the whole image looked like a funeral.

"Thought you'd like it?"

Derek raised his eyebrows, amused. "Do I seem that dour?"

"You have not brought me joy," Sebastian replied without hesitation. After a beat, Derek burst out into a hearty laugh; the genuine nature almost made Sebastian join in. He glowered instead. He couldn't understand why he was here or why he was being made fun of. Of course, he gave Derek that image. It was awful, and just the thought of it reminded him of everything he wanted to forget. Everything that, all of a sudden, he couldn't stop himself from remembering.

"I'd forgotten about the topiaries," Derek said. "I remember asking Manny to make one into a cat head, and he just growled at me."

Sebastian's heart skipped, not once but twice. He looked up and stared at Derek. He felt like he was seeing him properly for the first time. The sandy hair, darker now, as it does when you age, but the eyes, the eyes were still clear and almost sparkling. It was hard to tell without the hero worship in them, but they were the same. Derek smiled at him but said nothing, allowing all the pieces to come together in Sebastian's mind on their own. Sebastian, for his part, didn't move, didn't cry, didn't blink, but just stared. He tried to picture this grown man, handsome and crafty, cowering behind a pair of woman's legs.

"Brian?"

The smile on Derek's face grew, and he clapped his hands together. "Yup, and I know you have a lot of questions, but first," he jumped out of his chair and left the room. Sebastian heard a drawer open and then the banging of someone trying too quickly to close it again. By the time Derek returned, he was nearly running, and he slid across the kitchen floor and landed in the chair. He slammed something metal down on the table. "Look."

When Derek lifted his hand away, Sebastian saw a small coin, rusted in spots but definitely not American. He picked it up and saw the profile of a mustachioed man surrounded in Latin. He had no idea what he was looking at or what it said, but one thing was certain. This man who gave him the coin was, without a doubt, definitely Brian.

"You said there was treasure down there, and you were right. Though I'm pretty sure Manny just hid it there."

The sound of water rushing into the dark echoed in his ears. He smelled the mud and damp ferns that surrounded the cave entrance. He felt his socks soaking up the rain and the wet spread along his backside as he sat there, clutching Brian's bag. He'd only just relived this moment with Angela, mourning all over for the boy he thought he'd lost forever.

Sebastian didn't understand what grace led him here, at this kitchen table with the smell of charring roast filling the air. It would be too easy to say a weight had been lifted off of the professor; more like he had been lifted out of the dark and out of the very cave he thought he'd lost his first friend. 'His first love,' his heart reminded him. Sebastian thanked God that he was all cried out. He dropped the coin, grabbed Derek's hand, and laughed.

16

SEBASTIAN LAUGHED until his cheeks flared hot. As he calmed down, he patted the back of Derek's hand, or was it Brian's hand, and wondered which question to start with. He was confused and relieved, and there was a small sense of annoyance creeping in. The relief he felt at having his strange feelings confirmed was like sunlight shining on his whole existence. He knew what had sparked all those memories after all this time. He sat there, silent, the laughter no longer covering the awkwardness of the situation. Thankfully, Derek started first.

"Derek is my middle name. I started going by it when I left for college."

Sebastian nodded. As good a place to start as any. "And Morton?"

"That was my," Derek said and took a long pull of his drink, "my father's name." He chuckled, but there was no joy in that laugh. "I have a lot of backstories for you."

Sebastian let his shoulders slump a bit and ran his fingers through his hair. What he thought was going to be an annoying evening was turning out to be revelatory. "I think I'm going to need a drink then."

Derek nodded and headed for the counter. Sebastian added, "Also, some of that barbecue. I'm starving."

***

WITH THE DIRTY dishes pushed to the side and the bottles of liquor conveniently brought to the table, Sebastian felt full and light at the same time. Unfortunately, the more of Derek's story he heard, the angrier he felt. He also noticed something missing, something his old friend was holding back.

"Your mother seemed to have wrecked both of us. I really thought you were dead this whole time."

"That was the point," Derek said, spinning his tumbler. "There was no way she was going to get custody of me, and she used the accident as a way of hiding me." Sebastian looked down at Derek's right arm. He could see the thin scar that ran from his wrist up past his elbow. "How many surgeries?"

"Two when I was still a kid. One more at 20. Hurts like hell when it rains, but still works." He flexed his arm and punched the air. Sebastian took a quick sip of his scotch to cover the blush that flooded his neck and cheeks. He'd probably had a bit too much to drink, and he wasn't looking forward to another night in his office. He leaned forward. "She convinced me that I had taken you from her. What kind of bitch does that to a kid?"

"Hey," Derek said, "that's my mother you're talking about."

Sebastian was about to apologize when a sly smile broke on Derek's face. "I haven't spoken to her in years. My father hasn't heard from her either. For all I know, she's dead. Once her scheme was uncovered, she vanished."

Sebastian tried to remember the woman's name and couldn't. He thought about the moment he saw her posing naked for Shaw. The image of her standing there serenely didn't match with the woman who came to his room and destroyed him. He wondered if she was the reason he felt distaste for women like her. He wondered if he'd ever tell Derek his secret. Sebastian looked up, his eyes sleepy from the alcohol, and looked at the man's handsome face. He gulped before he could stop himself.

Derek smiled like a dream.

"Should I call you Brian? I don't know how it would sound."

Derek reached out his hand. "My father doesn't call me that, but you can. You'd be the only one who calls me that." He laced his fingers lightly with Sebastian's. "I'd like that."

Alcohol and relief settled on Sebastian. The end-of-semester pressures and the news about his probation seemed to melt together. He squeezed Derek's hand and remembered.

"Ah," he said, sitting up and letting go. "I forgot that we have business. Well, what we actually have is a problem." Sebastian took a few deep breaths. "Bri... Mr. Morton, I think I have to take some time to assess what my next moves are." He got up, gently, and grabbed his bag. He looked at his host. Derek looked disappointed but made no move to stop him. "I have a lot to think about, and while I am so very grateful to...to know you again, we are, unfortunately, on opposite sides of a conflict." He grasped the strap with both hands and breathed slowly. He had to make sure he was sober enough to get out of the house without incident.

"Thank you for the dinner," Sebastian said, without looking back, "but I should go."

He made it to the entryway when Derek grabbed his arm from behind. He turned Sebastian around and backed him into the wall. He leaned into him, barring him from moving without touching him. Derek stared for a moment and moved his face close. "I am going to kiss you now," he said. He waited. Sebastian knew this was his moment to refuse, to push him away, to say no, but he stood there. He was seeing Brian and Derek at the same time, and before his brain could figure out what was happening, Derek's lips touched his.

Sebastian had expected it to be forceful, insistent, like his personality, but Derek was gentle, testing to see how long he could linger there. Sebastian's heart raced, and he felt a mixture of confusion and submission. With each passing moment, he was giving in, letting Derek know that he wanted this. Just as Sebastian dropped his bag, Derek pulled away.

They held each other's gaze for a beat, and then Derek said, "Open your mouth."

Sebastian had no strength to refuse. Derek's second kiss suggested that the first was from Brian, the boy, sweet and innocent. This was an adult kiss, his tongue circling around his own and gliding along the top of his mouth. Sebastian's knees started to shake, and for a moment, he was conscious of having never been kissed like this before. Not once. His heart broke for what he'd missed out on. Yet in a moment, Derek's unrelenting tongue tried to make up for lost time.

Sebastian, arms at his side and his back against the wall, had nowhere to go when Derek pushed himself forward. Derek's hands moved, and he pulled Sebastian closer. 'Ah,' Sebastian thought, 'He's hard. I can feel it.' He quickly realized that he was, too, and there was no way to hide it.

Sebastian grabbed his shoulders and pushed him away. Derek's face was bright red, and he seemed as flustered as Sebastian felt. That surprised him.

"I'm not sleeping with you to save my job," he said. It came out of nowhere, and he wasn't entirely sure why he said it. He needed something to slow down where this was going.

Derek took a step closer. "Would you sleep with me for another reason?"

He was nearly pulled back into him again, but the word "job" hung in the air, and no matter how close Derek got, no matter how long Sebastian stared at his face, his lips. Shit, he thought, the moment had passed. He dropped his hands and slid away from Derek.

"Good night," he said, grabbing his bag and heading for the front door. He wondered if Derek would stop him or call out to him. But he didn't, and Sebastian left the president's house confused, buzzed, and half-hard. Fucking hell, he thought and jogged to his car.

17

———————

DEREK KICKED the wall and swore.

"He got away," he said to the empty room. He thought about following, running after Sebastian, and trying to bring him back inside, but he realized it would be a bad play. From the moment he opened the door, the roles of president and professor fell away for Derek. It was only Sebastian and Brian here, all grown up, and no one in the way of them being together. He walked back into the kitchen to finish his drink and pour another. 'I suppose I dumped a bit too much on him,' he thought. Yet, the momentum carried him forward, and now he ran the risk of running right past the only thing he'd ever really worked toward. He picked up the coin and flipped it between his fingers, a trick he had learned in grad school. He'd fantasized once that he would reveal himself to Sebastian by nonchalantly flipping the coin like this, over and under his knuckles, until recognition shone on Sebastian's face, and they fell into each other's arms. Of course, that fantasy took place in a coffee shop in Paris where they'd happened to meet. When he interviewed for the job at Woodlawn, it was on the off chance that Sebastian was still in the area. He was surprised to find he taught here.

Derek swallowed another drink. The painting still sat in the corner where they'd left it. He assumed that the bad memories Sebastian had attached to it would fade once he learned the truth and who Derek really was. He was surprised to find him in Shaw's old office, though, with all the other coincidences running between their lives, it made sense. The man responsible for bringing them together in the first place would, indirectly, be the one to reunite them. Derek poured another drink and raised a glass to the dead man.

That was the drink that sent Derek into the den to sleep on the couch. He didn't want to sleep in his bed alone, not with the memory of Sebastian on his lips. In a way, he needed to punish himself for pushing too fast. In another way, he knew he'd never be able to navigate the stairs. He hoped Sebastian made it home okay.

He slipped into a drunk sleep, fitful and full of strange dreams. He woke once in the middle of the night, fully convinced he was a little boy and he was drowning. Derek fell off the couch, groaned, and spent the rest of the night on the floor as penance.

Sebastian slouched back to the art building, making sure to hug all the dark patches of the quad so nosy presidents couldn't laugh at him from their windows. He stumbled into his office and used the light of his phone to navigate around the piles of books and boxes. He didn't want to advertise that he was there. At the far end of the room, he sat on a small table and stared out the window that faced the president's house. He could see into a room and beyond that the entranceway where... He unconsciously touched his mouth, and chills ran down his neck. The lights were still on, but it was a while before he saw Derek moving around, into the visible room. He stood for a moment and then flopped down, Sebastian assumed onto a sofa. He watched for a while longer but saw nothing. 'This is too close to stalking,' he told himself, still looking.

Confusion and weariness were getting the best of him, and he moved over toward his desk. The puffy chair he kept for reading served as a makeshift bed, and he set the alarm on his phone for six, early enough to sneak off campus. His heavy eyes tried to figure out the shapes in the dark room, and for a moment, he fixated on the remaining paintings he hadn't sent with Casey. None of them were remarkable or mysterious or gave Sebastian any emotional trauma. They were just good landscapes and still lifes. More than passable pieces of art. The remnants of his mentor's work. Sebastian blinked slowly and yawned, sleep overtaking him. He wondered what he would leave behind. What things of his could be stacked so neatly? What, if anything, had he created?

"Nothing," came his voice, thick and low. "Nothing," and he drifted off.

18

SEBASTIAN, *12 years old*

Sebastian waited in the garden; his book lay forgotten on the bench. He heard the crunching of Manny's feet in the gravel, and dark memories threatened to take him. He needed to remain hopeful and open. He needed to be the grateful and normal twelve-year-old boy. If he could get his one wish, he knew he could pull himself out of this darkness forever.

"Seb," Manny spoke softly from the edge of the path. He looked up and saw the extra grey in the groundskeeper's beard and the soft lines around the eyes. "He's ready for you." He smiled and held out a large, calloused hand. Sebastian was still on the child-side of twelve and instinctively took it. They walked cautiously back to the manor house, looking like the oddest and saddest set of twins. One large man and one young boy, both dressed in black. This small procession had the look of a life-changing event.

"How are you, son?" Campbell Shaw said, getting up from his desk. Most of the visitors had left after the memorial service. Beverly and Manny had spared Sebastian most of the gathering, keeping him in the kitchen or out in the garden. Some of the mourners found him, those closest to his parents, and cried over him. Others just looked out the manor's windows and wondered what would become of him. Ella and Harold Tate had taken care of that years ago, after their first summer with Shaw, but he'd overheard some arguments on his father's side of the family, distant cousins that thought differently. In the blink of an eye, Sebastian's parents were gone, and suddenly, he was here at his new home.

"Okay, I guess." Sebastian watched the man's face and assumed he answered wrong. "Of course, I'm sad, sir," he said. "But right now, I'm okay."

Shaw smiled, and Sebastian relaxed. He had never really developed a close relationship with the painter, and after Brian, he didn't think it was a good idea to get close to anyone. Life had a way of taking away the people he cared about the most. He squeezed Manny's hand and held back a sob. "There is nothing I can say to take away your pain. I'm sorry about that. But that pain is a testament to your parents and their love for you," Shaw said and, after a pause, added, "and their love for each other." Sebastian's forehead wrinkled, and his eyes became blurry. He could feel his hand slipping from Manny's grip, and all at once, he found himself running to the man seated behind the desk. He saw Shaw's arms open, and he flung himself onto the man's lap and sobbed.

At some point, Beverly had brought them drinks and snacks. The next thing he knew, he was lying on the office sofa, wrapped in a blanket. It was nighttime, and a fire gave the room a festive feeling with its flickering warmth. He sat up and saw Manny and Beverly talking in the hallway. Beverly was wiping her eyes, and Manny had his arm around her shoulder. Sebastian watched them amazed. He'd never seen such affection between the two people before. Manny always teased Beverly, and she would always snap her towel at him to get him out of the kitchen. He thought they were coworkers and friends. However, Sebastian understood there was more to this relationship and, more importantly, that this moment wasn't meant to be seen.

He verified this when he heard Shaw coming down the stairs. The couple released their embrace and moved a couple of feet away from each other, like a step perfected by veteran dancers. Sebastian felt shame having witnessed their intimate moment. That shame felt familiar, and a memory started to emerge from the darkness. When Shaw entered the office, the feeling disappeared. "Ah, you are awake." Shaw sat down on the edge of the sofa and smoothed out the boy's hair. "It's a cool night, but clear. Do you want to go for a walk?"

Sebastian unwrapped himself from the blanket and stretched. Still sleepy, he stared at the fire and wondered if he had the energy for a walk.

"I can ask Beverly to have two large cups of cocoa ready for us when we return. How's that?"

Sebastian nodded. "Sure," he mumbled and slowly got to his feet. The two passed Beverly and Manny in the hallway, both smiling at the boy, and headed out through the French doors off the long dining room. A thin brick patio ran along the back of the house, ending in another gravel driveway with several footpaths leading off into the flower and vegetable gardens and fields. Shaw led them into the fields, the better to see the night sky without cover. They walked for a while, not saying a word; the pathway was clear in the light of the full moon. The grass took on a silvery tone, and the tree line, that marked the forest entrance to the east, shimmered.

"Sebastian," Shaw stopped walking but didn't turn

around, "I want you to know that I cannot replace your parents, but I will fulfill my promise and provide a home for you."

Sebastian wasn't sure what to say in the pause, so he relied on still being a child and said a small "Thank you."

Shaw turned around. "I am not doing this out of charity but out of a real affection for you and your family. I cannot be a loving father or mother, but perhaps I can be a guide or mentor." Shaw looked as if he had thought about this speech for a while, but his face betrayed his uncertainty to Sebastian. The boy decided to stay quiet, letting the man talk.

"I think you have a lot of opportunities here, and you should make the most of this situation. I can provide you with a top-notch education and opportunities." He knelt and put his hands on the boy's shoulders. "Whatever you want to learn or try, I will help you," Shaw said, the control in his voice breaking. He looked down at the ground. "There has been too much loss already," he said, and Sebastian felt he was talking about Brian.

It was the first time Shaw even said anything remotely related to his friend. Sebastian had always felt that Shaw blamed him for Brian's death, that Brian had been special, and that Sebastian had taken him away. But Brian had been special, special to Sebastian, and he felt a combination of guilt and jealousy over Shaw's unwillingness to mourn his friend. The tears that were threatening again fell on Sebastian's face, and he started shuddering with each sob. Shaw looked up, and Sebastian could tell he'd been crying as well.

"We will keep each other well and safe," Shaw said, digging his fingers into the boy's shoulders. "Tell me what I can do for you."

Sebastian didn't know. He didn't know what he wanted or

what he needed. That's what parents were for. He hadn't gotten over losing Brian, and the only two people who knew how much he'd hurt were dead. Now, here was Shaw, kneeling in the dirt, crying, asking him what to do. Shaw, the famous painter who owned the big house. Shaw, the college professor who also wrote books. Shaw, the smartest and scariest adult that Sebastian had ever known, was asking a twelve-year-old boy what to do?

He didn't know. He didn't know anything. The only thing he could be sure of was that right over Shaw's shoulder was the path that, if you followed it east, would lead you to the cave where Sebastian's hopes died along with his best friend. What he needed was a parent. What he needed was an adult to tell him what to do. What he needed was an outlet.

Shaw stood and, like a child, ran the sleeve of his suit over his nose. He wiped the dirt off of his knees and looked up at the moon. "Let's go back," he said, looking back down at Sebastian. "I can almost taste the cocoa."

They were almost at the gravel driveway when Sebastian tugged on Shaw's suit jacket, making him stop. "What is it, son? What's wrong?"

Sebastian thought for a moment and then straightened his shoulders, looking directly into Shaw's face. "I figured out what you can do for me."

"Anything. Tell me."

Sebastian took a deep breath. "Teach me how to paint like you."

Shaw's smile rivaled the moon for brightness that night. "Yes, Sebastian. I think I will."

They walked into the warm glow of the kitchen and wordlessly enjoyed their large mugs of cocoa.

19

Sebastian got up with the sun, having neglected to pull the blinds down in his office. His first glance was out the far window, across the quad to the president's house. He doubted there would be movement there this early, and in the brightness of the day, it would largely be invisible to him, anyway. He scratched his scalp and pried himself off the chair, letting the overcoat that served as his blanket fall to the floor. The evening had left him confused and annoyed, and he felt that his office should reflect his mood. He stood in front of his coffee pot for a long time, willing it to set itself up. Thankfully, the physical memory of that kiss had faded, but the emotional memory still held strong. For the first time in his life, he wanted a terrific hangover, the kind that makes thinking hurt. He didn't want to think now. He grabbed the carafe. Sebastian didn't want to think anymore.

With the determination of a man saying "water, water" over and over in his head, he walked right past Casey, who was sitting outside his office. A few more steps and a strange sensation made Sebastian turn around. The kid was sitting on a wooden bench, head tilted back against the wall, and sleeping. He wore a neon green t-shirt and cargo shorts, looking like a displaced beach bum. The kid's brown curls hung all around his face, and Sebastian thought he must be popular with women. He sneered at the kid, then slumped. "Hey," he called out. Casey didn't move.

He tried again. "Hey, kid!"

Casey jolted forward so fast he over-corrected and slammed the back of his head against the wall. "AH! Dr. Tate. Hi. Ow!"

Sebastian tried to scratch his head again, nearly braining himself with the coffee carafe in his hand. He grunted and turned back down the hall without another sound.

"Oh, should I just wait?"

In answer, Sebastian lifted the carafe again. 'Fuck if I care,' he thought, then thought that Casey could distract him at least for a short time.

While Sebastian made coffee, Casey made himself at home in the office. "You stayed here again," he said, more of a statement than a question.

"Why are you here so early on a Saturday during break?"

"Ah," Casey sat up. "Oh, would it be okay if I had some coffee, too?"

Sebastian frowned and shrugged. "Fine. What do you want...besides coffee?"

"Yes, I wanted your answer about teaching me this summer. I really need to be in your class this fall."

It took Sebastian a moment to remember this dilemma, and all at once, the kid's request came back to him. He looked skeptical. "Is it a girl?"

"Nope," was the immediate reply. Casey offered nothing more. Sebastian was starting to get his wish. His head throbbed.

"Can you pull down some of those shades?" he asked, needing to get some of the brightness out of the room. "Not that one," he said when Casey was at the far end of the office. Casey looked out the window and then back at Sebastian. If a knowing look passed across the young man's face, it was lost on the professor whose eyes suddenly decided to betray him and pulse in time with his heartbeat.

"Better?"

"Yes."

"So, this summer..." Casey's anticipation was nearly as bright as the sun and just as off-putting.

"Look," Sebastian said, turning toward his desk and leaning on a scattering of papers. On top were the preliminary minutes of the College of Arts meeting. His throbbing eyes picked out the line "How many students are in your major now?" He remembered Derek's face in the meeting, the face of Derek the businessman, or Derek the vulture. He certainly couldn't be the same Derek from last night. Derek, who was Brian. Derek the kisser.

"Seven," he'd answered and was proud of the number because he was proud of his students. Four were heading into top-tier graduate schools. That's over half his students. But seven. He'd said seven, and the room was silent. No one stood up for seven. Not the Dean, not Willoughby. To be brutally honest, not even Sebastian could defend seven. This year, only five people were majoring in the arts. The class Casey was so desperate to be in only had three registered students so far. Anything under six meant the class would have to be canceled.

Sebastian tried to slap his forehead but only succeeded in swatting at his nose.

He stood, grabbed two mugs, blew dust off the unused one, and poured two coffees. He returned, handed Casey a mug, and watched him over his own steaming cup. "I can waive the prerequisites, but that doesn't mean you won't be studying over the summer."

Casey sat up in his chair. "Yes. I will work my ass off."

"Not just you."

"Eh?"

Sebastian sipped his coffee, trying desperately to quell the trembling in his hands. He'd wished himself a whopper of a hangover, and it was well on its way. "I'm not going to do a bunch of extra work to get one more butt in a seat this fall." He sipped again. "You're on a sports team, right?"

"Lacrosse," he said.

"Good team?"

Casey offered up a hesitant "yes."

Sebastian nodded. "Bring at least four more, for the summer work and to enroll in the fall, then I'll agree to it."

Casey's mouth fell open. He closed it, his eyes darting back and forth as if reading an internal team roster. After a moment, Casey appeared to have his starters. "Agreed. When do we start?"

Sebastian held up a hand. "I don't want a bunch of slackers. And no signing up for the course just to drop. Got it?"

Casey meant to say something, then changed his mind. He nodded his understanding.

"Let's start two weeks from Monday. We can meet in here."

Casey stood up and leaned over to shake Sebastian's hand. "Thank you so much, Dr. Tate. You won't regret it."

He waved the kid away. "Fine, just email the list of names and leave me the hell alone until then."

Casey took a final swig of his coffee and jogged out of the office. He was mindful enough not to slam the door.

Sebastian leaned back in his chair and nursed his coffee. For a while, he stared out the far window and watched the house. Sometimes, when his head didn't throb or his eyes didn't burn, he'd wonder what was going on in there. Mostly, he wondered what was going on inside Derek's mind and what had happened to his young friend to have changed so much.

After finishing the pot of coffee, he slipped out of the office and drove to Shaw Manor. He pulled onto the gravel drive and tried to picture it as the first time he'd seen it. So many familiar things can only become new through someone else's eyes. How he wanted to tear the whole thing apart to find all of its secrets. Someone knocked on his window. Sebastian rolled it down.

"Is this a proper time to come home?" Beverly said. She was carrying a small satchel of produce. "Want some breakfast?"

He slowly got out of the car. "Yeah, Beverly. Thanks." She unlocked the door, and Sebastian followed the housekeeper inside.

20

Derek burned the first three pancakes he tried to make. He gave up and ate an orange. He'd woken up in the middle of the night and had the forethought to drink a tall glass of water and take three aspirins, so the effects of his drunkenness didn't linger into the morning. He sat at the kitchen table and stared at the seat Sebastian had been in less than 12 hours before and replayed the evening in his head. Over the years, he had so many scenarios, so many fantasies about finally seeing Sebastian and revealing who he was, that it had happened over this wooden table seemed disappointing. He'd built up the reunion so high in his mind and had wanted to see him again for so long that there was probably no reality that would live up to his dreams. He leaned forward on the table, spreading his arms across it as if to reach for the person who had just been there. "Ugh," he said and pressed his chin into the varnished wood.

He opened one eye and looked at the painting in the corner. Casey had said something about it being weird, but when he inspected it, Derek could see the odd angles. From that distance, about ten feet, the painting seemed like an unassuming architectural portrait. The red brick of the Shaw Manor dominated the first two-thirds of the scene, coming in from the left. The topiaries that lined the front under the window were painted with grayish green, not reflecting their natural verdant coloring. (He didn't think Manny would have appreciated the switch.) Curving in from the bottom was the gravel drive. The iron arch and gate that lead to the gardens filled the final third of the painting. Derek couldn't remember clearly but thought the ivy and ferns that lined the fencing and the gate were a little heavy, and he didn't remember there being so much honeysuckle climbing the arch. Even so, it felt familiar. In his amateur opinion, the entire scene was passable, even pretty well done, but not something terribly inspiring without firsthand knowledge of the place or the painter.

When Derek moved to the area this spring, he'd driven by the Shaw Manor on more than one occasion, too nervous to actually turn down the drive. One evening in March, he thought he saw light in the windows, but this was after he realized Sebastian was teaching at his new school, and the building became only a passing curiosity. He tried to list out all the coincidences that led him back here. There was no way to get a clear trace on his good luck, but it would be naïve of Derek to think he hadn't been looking for a place to open at Woodlawn. Campbell Shaw had been a popular professor here, and even if Sebastian was on the other side of the world looking for adventure, there was a connection here that Derek could build upon. Finding Sebastian teaching at the same college, even using the same office as Shaw, wasn't nearly as surprising as the drastic change in his personality.

He first spotted him during his interview when the two passed each other in the student union building. Derek did a double-take, unconvinced that the sullen man with the shoulder-length black hair and a preoccupied aura was the same person.

"That's our arts professor, Dr. Tate. He took over for Campbell Shaw. He's a bit, ah, dark, but that seems to fit him."

'No,' Derek remembered thinking as he watched Sebastian walk away. 'That doesn't fit him at all. I knew him. He was the most confident and powerful person in the world.' That night, Derek returned to his hotel and seriously considered withdrawing his application for the president's job. He knew he was in the top three; the deans were very easy to read, but he wasn't sure he could stand his disillusionment. That night, he drove past the manor house for the first time in a while. From the street, he could just make out the half-moon window of the attic. There was no doubt in his mind that he knew the real Sebastian Tate.

Looking at the painting, he noticed that one of the upstairs windows was lit up, Shaw having painted it with a lighter gray than the others. Derek moved over to the chair next to the canvas and looked closer. He used the flash on his phone, and peering closely at the window, Derek thought he could see a shape up there, as if there was a person looking out at the painter. The light caught all the ridges and valleys of the oil paint, dissolving the illusion of a flat image. He had never spent time looking this closely at a painting and wondered if this was part of Sebastian's life, this detailed work. He liked the idea of Sebastian worrying less about the picture and more about this particular blob of green or this tiny swirl of orange in the honeysuckle. He thought about how the closer you got to a painting, the more you see of its beginning and the less of its end. It was like traveling back in time.

As he ran the bright LED light over the garden gate, Derek noticed another unusual shape. Instead of a mysterious figure in color, this was a mysterious figure in relief. The orange and greens of the honeysuckle seemed much thicker than the surrounding oils. Here and there, large clumps of paint had little of the delicate swirling patterns of other areas like the front of the house or even the strange window. But here, there was a buildup of color, which, while not obvious from the front, was unmistakable at this distance. He carefully ran the tip of his finger over the topography and thought he could discern an outline. He caressed and retraced the area.

Derek sat back in the chair, shining the light directly on the honeysuckle vine and the iron gate. He was almost positive that there had been the figure of a person underneath all that orange and green. Shaw Campbell had taken the time to paint over someone he originally painted in front of his home. He wondered if there was a way to find out who it was.

Derek chuckled to himself, remembering that he had a full-time art history professor on staff. Of course, there was the inconvenient fact that he'd just threatened that full-time job and that he'd just chased him out of his house by kissing him. He sighed, still looking at the iron gate. 'I have to know,' he thought. 'And it's a good excuse to see him again.'

21

SEBASTIAN PROVED to be a difficult man to find, and for all of Derek's wanderings on campus, he never ran into the professor—not even when he hung around the arts building, getting suspicious looks from Angela in the main office. And especially not when he just gave up and sat outside on the lawn, directly in front of Sebastian's office window, reading a book on Van Gogh. After a week, as he drank bitter coffee in the student union, he chastised himself for acting like a love-struck kid and wondered if he was mature enough to be the president of a university. As he questioned his life choices, a loud voice called to him from the corridor. "Ah, Dr. Morton! I am so happy to run into you!"

Derek's ability to hide a groan while throwing a wide smile was a key to his success, and as the Dean of Business shuffled over to take the seat opposite of him, he realized his whole morning was about to be monopolized. "Good morning, Dean. And please call me Derek. I'm not a PhD."

"Yes, yes, Derek. I keep forgetting," he said, with the understanding that he had indeed not forgotten. He plopped down in the vinyl seat opposite, which made a hilarious noise. "I have a few things I would like to go over with you about our new majors and how it may have an impact on fundraising. Do you have time now?" He pulled out a personal tablet from his brief-case and started flipping through screens.

Derek agreed. While he hadn't anticipated a slide presenta-tion over his morning latte, the distraction might be good for him and, well, he did have a job to do. This weekend would be his first fundraiser with alumni, and this information might be helpful. He took a deep breath and felt a little thankful for the dean. His face must have betrayed him.

"Oh," he said, "looks like you're really interested. Let me grab a coffee, and we can talk at our leisure." He left with a "puff" as the air went back into the seat cushion. Derek muted his phone, taking one last look to see if there was any word from Sebastian. His notifications were all college-related emails. He put it face down on the table and waited for the dean.

Three hours later, Derek had a backache and a list of "revo-lutionary ideas" from the Dean of Business. The man had apparently been stockpiling his thoughts until, as he had said, "a more forward-thinking president came along." On his way out of the student union, he passed the portrait of Henry Menkin, the last president of Woodlawn. Menkin presided over the school for a record forty years and made it his mission to keep the small liberal arts college focused on its core goal: creating well-rounded, critical, and thoughtful citizens. Derek understood that he represented a new direction for the school and one that would face a great deal of resistance. He believed that Woodlawn deserved to stay relevant in the 21st century, yet if it stayed just a small, liberal arts college, it would quickly be overtaken by larger institutions and vocationally focused colleges. A lot of the surrounding area's best and brightest were heading out of state to some of the smaller ivies or were swallowed up by the big state university an hour away. Walking across the quad, Derek wondered if he could bring in more donor money by selling Woodlawn as a physical experience as well as an intellectual one. Perhaps he could pull back some of the harsher cuts.

Even with the sun at its highest, the shade of the elms outside the art building brought a welcome relief. Derek paused, staring at the sign on the brick wall of the building. He'd been lost in his thoughts and ended up here, on the other side of campus. He had no indication that Sebastian was in his office, but here he was, just outside. A few more steps down the walk and he'd be right outside his office window. He kept staring at the sign, not wanting to betray what he was thinking. He went over to the wooden bench on the far side of the walkway and sat. There was certainly nothing unusual about the new president meandering around his new campus. 'In fact,' he thought, 'it should be completely normal since my house is right there.' He sipped his cooling latte and closed his eyes, listening to the light rustling of the leaves, the finches, and a far-off woodpecker. In this cool spot, he could sense the hundreds and thousands of students that must have passed by over time. A campus held onto some of that anxiety and excitement in the same way old buildings hold on to trauma. He thought he could write a story of Woodlawn that would showcase this feeling. He could sell the story of Woodlawn right from this bench.

The sound of footsteps tore him out of his meditation. Derek opened his eyes to see a group of young men staring at him from the sidewalk.

"Hey, Pres," Casey Stanfield said, smiling, "Having a good day?"

"Hi, Casey. What are you all doing here? You should be enjoying your break."

A couple of the men groaned, but Casey admonished them. "Hey now. We just finished in the league tournament. We're usually on campus a little late."

Derek nodded. "I'm sorry, I should know that. How did your team do?"

Every single one of them looked down and shifted back and forth. "Well," Casey, official lacrosse spokesman said, "we were seeded pretty low to begin with. But", he held up his index finger, "we have some very exciting freshmen coming in this fall. So, I have a lot of hope for next season." He smiled, and Derek could understand why these other four boys were following Casey around. If he were about 15 years younger, so would he.

"I look forward to the Woodlawn lacrosse team being league champions next year," Derek said, standing up. "I'll see you gentlemen around campus."

"Yes, we have to go to class now. See you." Casey and the boy closest both waved; the others nodded. As they entered the building, Derek caught one of them saying "art history," and he stopped in his tracks. He turned and looked at the sign again. Only one person would be teaching art history, and it would be the one person he's spent a week searching for. He weighed the pros and cons of bursting in on a class and creating an awkward atmosphere. He didn't think the other team members would understand, but Derek was pretty sure Casey knew something was up. The kid was too smart by half. He stood there, worrying. Even the woodpecker took a break to let him think.

"Dammit," he said, heading straight for the door. "I want to see him."

Outside, the soft click of the arts building door was lost in the sound of the woodpecker resuming its business.

22

DEREK STOOD IN A DESERTED HALLWAY, listening for the sound of five young men heading to class. There wasn't a peep, nor a footfall, not even a disgruntled murmur. 'Nothing. He hadn't been long in following them into the building, so they couldn't have gone far,' he thought. He decided the best plan was to start at Sebastian's office. As cluttered and messy as it was, surely, he could fit five guys in there for a small class. It would be close quarters. How close? Derek broke out into a jog.

Sebastian's office was tucked into the corner of the first floor. The door was shut, and there was no way to tell if a light was on inside. He hung close to the side of the door, not wanting his shadow to be seen through the frosted glass. Derek held his breath and listened for voices. He heard nothing and then took a moment to mock himself for his skittish behavior. He was the president of this university, and he could go into any room he damn well pleased.

He knocked lightly on the glass. There was no reply. He tried the handle, but the door was locked. Derek sighed and stood looking at the words "Arts Department" in peeling letters on the door. He made a mental note to have the facilities department come freshen this up. Then he remembered that he'd put Sebastian's position on probation. "Whatever," he said to himself and decided to explore the rest of the building for no reason at all. If he happened to run into Sebastian teaching a bunch of athletes the difference between Manet and Monet, so be it.

The arts building held not just the arts department but the history department and modern languages. Each department had its own floor, with the arts department sharing the first floor with a writing center, tutoring classrooms, and a language lab. By the time Derek reached the Spanish faculty offices, he was slightly out of breath and out of rooms to check. He sat in a folded chair outside an office. He talked to those kids, right? He watched them come into the building, right? Where the hell was everyone?

He felt defeated and frustrated, and even if Sebastian was right around the next corner, Derek didn't think his current mood would yield a good conversation. He spied the elevator at the end of the hallway and decided to ride back down to the first floor to head home. It was an old-style elevator, fashioned behind a regular door. Once inside, Derek had to pull a metal gate closed before selecting a floor. He looked at the control pad, the large black buttons sticking out of the brass metal plate. Most of the white numbers had worn away, but Derek could plainly read the capital "B" on the bottom button. He hooked his fingers into the diamond-shaped opening of the gate. 'Might as well,' he thought and pressed B.

The elevator moved hesitantly. When he passed the doors of the second and first floors, he could see the hallways beyond the door. He noticed there wasn't a way to call for help if the elevator became stuck. He made another mental note to find out if this was up to code. Everyone had a cell phone on them anyway, he figured, but he didn't want any trouble down the road. The elevator slowed and then jolted to a halt. When Derek looked out through the gate, all he saw was blackness.

He slid the gate to the side and opened the door. The smell of mildew hit him full in the face. He stepped into a dimly lit hallway. To his right was a dead end, much like the other floors. To his left was a long corridor, hooded lamps hanging low from the ceiling. The fourth lamp from where he stood flickered. 'I'm going to get murdered down here,' he thought. He took a few tentative steps down the hallway when he heard a scream. He broke into a run, recognizing Sebastian's voice almost instantly. He saw light spilling into the hallway from a room on the left. He nearly slid past it as he made the turn. Derek burst in to see Casey in the middle of the room, holding Sebastian in his arms.

Frustration, exhaustion, and confusion all mixed together to give Derek a completely wrong read on the situation. He lunged forward and pushed Casey aside, knocking him onto his backside. He grabbed Sebastian's arm and pushed him toward the far wall, pinning him there with his back to him as if shielding the professor. He took two breaths and realized the other four were in the room, seated as if they'd been watching Casey and Sebastian. A projection screen had been pulled down on the opposite side of the room, and high in the center of the ceiling, the control panel of the video projector hung open. His breathing slowed, tension leaving his body.

"I'm going to assume you've just figured out what happened," Sebastian said from behind him. Derek moved away and let Sebastian walk around him and return to the center of the room. He pointed to the projector. "Mr. President, it would be great if we could get these in a few more class-rooms. And preferably projectors that don't need constant maintenance." He helped Casey to his feet and repositioned the step-stool the young man had just tripped over. Derek felt dazed but automatically went over to Sebastian to see that he didn't fall. Sebastian replaced the panel on the underside of the projector before Derek got close.

"A moment of your time, Mr. Morton," Sebastian said, stepping lightly off the stool. Derek followed him out into the hallway, like a child ready to be scolded by his teacher.

23

THE HALL FELT CRAMPED AND, had this been later in the summer, would have held onto the dampness that was one of Pennsylvania's charming little secrets. Sebastian thought for a moment, trying to decide how to begin. He didn't want to look at Derek, not just yet. His own embarrassment from that little scene in the classroom hadn't subsided, and he didn't want Derek to misunderstand. He shook his head and felt entirely too old to even think of a word like that.

"Look, just give me a minute," Sebastian finally said, backing away. He leaned against the opposite wall and was thankful to see that Derek hadn't moved with him. Sebastian looked up into the face of a man earnestly sorry for his actions. He could see all the words Derek wanted to say and thought if he gave this guy an opening, a torrent of emotion would drown them both. "First, I'm not mad," Sebastian offered.

Derek relaxed, letting out a long breath he'd been holding, and then remained silent. 'For all his impulsiveness, Sebastian thought, he had some awareness. You don't rise this high in academia at such a young age without it,' he thought.

"What's the emergency that you have to barge into the class?"

"I didn't even know you were teaching this summer. I just happened upon that group on their way here. You're not listed in the catalog." Derek kept his eye on Sebastian. "I checked."

Sebastian rubbed the back of his head and smiled. "Ah, this was a last-minute addition. Those guys," he pointed toward the closed classroom, "were pretty insistent and..." Sebastian wondered how much he should say. The main reason he was in this situation was Derek's own doing. Threatening the dissolution of his department made him agree to take this overload with the hope that they'd all sign up in the fall. He thought about Derek checking the summer class schedule. Did he think Sebastian was trying to play him? A quick stuffing of credits to make his department more important than the school thought it was. He looked back at Derek and saw no accusation in his face, no sign of disappointment. It made Sebastian madder.

"What does it matter? You have something you want to say to me, or can I go back to my class?" His shift in tone startled Derek, who took a step back and bumped into the wall. He was about to fold his arms, a gesture of confidence Sebastian had seen him pull in meetings, but he let his arms fall to his sides. Sebastian detected a note of defeat in the air.

"I needed your help with something," Derek said in a soft voice. "But I see I've overstepped." He cast his eyes up, looking back at Sebastian, like a boy unwilling to be scolded but knowing how much he deserved it.

The skin on Sebastian's nape broke out in goosebumps. In that moment, he looked so much like Brian he wondered how he never saw it in the first place. The blue eyes still held a trace of hero worship that he didn't deserve, not now and certainly not then. This kid before him, this man, was holding himself back for Sebastian's sake, and it simultaneously exited him and pissed him off. With a classroom full of lacrosse players in the next room, he chose pissed off, but regretted it the moment the words came out of his mouth.

"I'd appreciate it if you'd leave me alone right now. I take my teaching seriously." He held Derek's gaze longer than a professional relationship would require.

The president stood up straight, changing his demeanor instantly. "Understood, Dr. Tate. I look forward to seeing you this evening at my residence. Six o'clock. I'll have Angela put it on your calendar."

Sebastian smirked. What Derek wanted with him, well, he had a few ideas, but to make this official, to get Angela involved was just an abuse of power. He wouldn't be able to find a reasonable excuse at this late hour. Sebastian heard a shuffle from the other side of the classroom door and wondered if Derek was also performing for a group of eavesdroppers trying to get out of coursework. He opened his mouth to refuse the meeting when Derek added, "It has to do with a Campbell Shaw painting that has recently come into my possession."

Sebastian opened and closed his mouth. Obviously, it was in the group he'd sent, but none of them were particularly interesting or comment-worthy, except for one.

"There is an irregularity," Derek said and then nothing further. He stared with the singular intent of getting a message across: You will come to my house tonight.

Sebastian sighed, wanting to get this discussion, this class, this day, this whole damn summer over with. At least in the fall, he had enough business with the low-level classes to keep him distracted. The lazy, long days of summer usually left him in a sweaty depression of inactivity and disappointment. Now his summer was full of classes, jocks, and this guy. He looked at

Derek and stopped worrying about what kind of face he was making. He had a feeling he knew what it was: resignation, exhaustion, confusion, all the emotions that make up "Why now?" There was too much floating between them at that moment, too much lost history and too much potential pain. Sebastian felt the walls of the hallway narrowing, pulling him closer to Derek. He stared at those big blue eyes again and realized why he was anxious.

The closer Sebastian got to Derek, the further he felt from Brian.

"I'll talk to you later, Dr. Tate." Without a glance back, Derek entered the stairwell at the far end of the corridor. The metal latch of the door echoed. It sounded like a smack to Sebastian's face.

"Dammit," he said, walking back into the classroom. Casey and company were where he'd left them, chatting about practice. The standing boys took their seats, and Sebastian grabbed the projectors' remote. "Sorry for the interruption. Let's start at the beginning." The screen filled with a photo of a cave interior, the wall a striation of browns and reds, and across the wide space, a distant hand had painted a thousand horses.

"Humanity has always painted," Sebastian lectured, falling easily into his teaching persona. "We paint what we see, and we paint what we want to see."

24

SEBASTIAN, *14 years old*

The room Shaw reserved for painting boasted the best light in the manor, and it was no surprise that he coveted his time there. Sebastian remembered the first time Shaw showed him to the room and a painting area set up just for him. His palms began to sweat, understanding the importance of being welcomed into this space. Previously, only Shaw's artist friends and the occasional model could breach the mahogany doors into the studio. Sebastian felt a chill at the thought of those models but couldn't give a specific reason why. The recent death of his parents occluded most of his childhood memories that didn't contain them. He was desperate to hold on to their images in his mind. As he crossed the room to look through all his new supplies, he wondered if he'd be able to paint them one day. He hoped he'd be good enough.

"I'll be starting you with the basics, and I'm afraid it will be a bit boring at first. No sweeping vistas, no eye-catching still lifes. This week, it's all about prepping your canvas and char-coal sketching." Shaw sat down in the comfortable chair by the fireplace and faced the boy. Sebastian nodded, looking at the stack of art books Shaw (or more likely Beverly) had left out for him. "Take a look at those in your free time, if you like. I've given you a good selection to start with."

Sebastian picked up the Picasso book first, eyeing the cubist painting *Three Musicians*. "I like this," he said. "It's like, all broken up."

"In a way." Shaw tilted his head to one side. "Some historians believe he was trying to paint from every angle at once."

Sebastian tilted the book back and forth as if trying to find the varying angles to the image. He almost understood what Shaw meant by "every angle at once," and his mind started filling with ideas of how many different views you could fit into one, flat image.

"Though, you need to get some convention before you can break it," Shaw said. "There's nothing simple about a simple landscape."

Sebastian sensed a strange tone in Shaw's voice that made him put down the book and look at his new guardian. "No, sir. I want to paint the way you paint. I just think it's," he glanced back at the book cover, "interesting."

Shaw's laugh dispersed any tension in the room, and the man stood up. He wasn't a very tall man and quite burly. He had the presence of an old sailor from Treasure Island, Sebastian thought. All he needed was a beard and a pipe, and he could picture him yanking in a fishing net. He giggled at himself, thinking it would be fun to paint a seascape with Shaw as the salty captain. He felt the man's hand on his shoulder. "Your father had quite a bit of talent, but talent is only part of it. If you want to do something, no amount of talent can replace practice and hard work."

Sebastian nodded, losing the smile on his face at the thought of his father.

"I tell you this not to discourage you but to give you hope. If you don't take to it easily, you can take to it hard. Put your back into it, as it were." Shaw looked past Sebastian to the scene beyond the two French doors. "Why don't we head out into the garden for a bit? Grab that sketch book and the pencil case, and let's see what we can see."

For the rest of the afternoon, Sebastian and Shaw wandered the grounds, occasionally stopping so Shaw could let him sketch, first a small shrub, then a bench. Near lunchtime, they sat on the grass near the tree line, and Sebastian attempted to draw Manny at work on a hedgerow. Shaw leaned over, "You may have an aptitude for figure drawing, though I think your sketch of the tractor has more personality." Sebastian shrugged, thinking how to respond. While Shaw had taken him in, showed him every kindness, even went out of his way to start private instruction, there was a lack of warmth in their relationship. Sebastian wasn't sure if the distance was due to the still strong presence of his parents or his unwillingness to replace them in his life with this man. He was also preoccupied with the start of a new school the following week, a private academy that intimidated his public school upbringing. He'd questioned Shaw about the decision. Had he been more confident like his mother, he would have argued against it, but Sebastian was too much like his father, a point Shaw brought up more frequently since he moved in.

"Harold would always sit here and sketch," he said, watching Manny haul the remains of a prickly bush into the trailer. "He loved landscapes, but he always sketched the small-scapes, these closer places that. How did he say it?" Sebastian watched him try to coax the memory out of the air. "Ah, landscapes are too big sometimes. Small-scapes are people level, and people are everything." Shaw chuckled and slowly stood up with a series of grunts and cracks.

"Your father was a good student, Seb. For as much as he liked people, he was terrible at faces." Sebastian sat on the ground, wanting to hear more about his father, hoping that Shaw could fill in some of the details of the world that were only tangential to his own. He felt glued to the grassy patch on which he sat, willing Shaw to say something, anything, more about his Dad. He struggled not to cry.

Shaw eventually added, "He was terrible at reading faces, too. I'm sure that's why..." He paused, looking down at the ground, and then brushed the grass and dirt off of his pants. "Well, let's go, Seb. I'm sure Beverly wishes for nothing more than to feed you. We can talk more later." Shaw headed back toward the house, not looking to see if the boy followed him.

Sebastian sat there for a while, thinking about that "why" and what it meant. Why wouldn't anyone tell him anything? This thought came from a new place, a dark place Sebastian only discovered after the funeral. Here was anger and grief and jealousy and all the emotions in life that his parents tried to keep from him, tried to protect him from. They worked so hard to make the world a good place for him that they didn't realize the real enemy was on the inside, and now, without them, with only this distant man to guide him into adulthood, Sebastian wasn't sure he'd have the strength to hold those feelings back. His eyes filled with tears.

25

SEBASTIAN, 14 years old

Sebastian looked down into his charcoal-stained hands and felt worse. If he wiped his face now, he'd just smear himself with the stuff, and nothing says to the world that you're still a kid than a dirty face. He stiffened when he heard the crunch of boots on dirt. He tried to wipe his face with the back of his sleeve. Manny's hulk blocked out the sun. "Allergies?"

Sebastian looked up into the kind face and allowed the tears to flow. He nodded. Manny sat down in the dirt and ruffled his hair. "Yeah, allergies are bad this time of year. Nothing you can do about it, son. Nothing at all."

By the time Sebastian arrived in the kitchen, Beverly was in a bit of a stir. As he walked in, the woman shoved him to the far end of the counter where his lunch waited and told him to eat quickly and get out of the way unless he wanted to help. "I've got ten guests coming tonight, and I need to get the place cleared up for the" and this last word she spat out like a curse, "caterer."

Sebastian swallowed a big bite out of an Italian hoagie and

asked, "What's going on? And why a caterer when you're here? You're the best cook ever."

Beverly blushed a bit at the compliment and patted the boy's hand. "Oh, you. Well, Mr. Shaw wants to make a particular impression on this group, it seems, and the ... caterer... is a former student."

Sebastian kept quiet, letting Beverly fill the silence with information. "Apparently, this is a fundraising opportunity for the college, and Mr. Shaw is their celebrity. The president normally has these functions at his home on campus, but he thinks the manor will make a bigger impression." She emptied the dishwasher and hastily stacked the plates into the cupboard. Sebastian quietly ate his sandwich. Beverly made the best hoagies.

"Between you and me, I think the president is trying to get this building for the college, maybe as the new presidential house."

Sebastian swallowed. "He's already got that big place on the quad, and this place isn't even near campus."

"Near enough," Beverly said, flapping a damp towel. "Mr. Shaw's been rattling around alone in this big house for years now. The last student he took in for private work was your father, and, dear, while it can't even compare to your loss, I think losing Harold really hurt him."

Sebastian expected his eyes to water again, but they didn't. Perhaps the time sitting with Manny helped get some of the sadness out of his system. He wondered if he would ever be completely free from the grief of losing them. He hoped not. Somehow, he felt that would disrespect them. What he didn't expect was what he said out loud. "You think it's my father he missed? Or my mother?"

Beverly stopped wiping down the far counter and stiffened.

She shifted her eyes to look at the boy but didn't turn her head. Sebastian watched her intently over the remains of his lunch, looking for any clue, any inkling of suspicion. Their eyes met, and Beverly suddenly relaxed and sighed loudly.

"Mr. Shaw has not always been gentlemanly to the ladies that stayed at the house, whether they were students or partners of his students." She moved closer and looked Sebastian square in the eye, making sure he could see her face and her intention. "Mr. Shaw regarded your mother with the utmost respect and never did anything foolish toward her. Harold was like a son to him, and she a daughter." She started wiping the counter again, falling back into a gossipy conversation. "Mind you, when the three of you first arrived, I was worried that he was going to act like a damn teenager," she smiled. "No offense, but I think he'd matured and had become much more concerned about the legacy of his work and teaching than fooling around."

Beverly brought out a half-iced cake from the fridge and cut off a thick slice. She slid the plate toward Sebastian, who nearly drooled at the sight of it. "You always get me gossiping. Here's my bribe. Don't you get me into trouble."

"My lips are sealed, Beverly. Thanks," Sebastian replied and dug into the cake. When she slid a glass of milk toward him, Sebastian could only manage a nod in thanks, his face filled with the chocolaty goodness of Beverly's baking. These moments in the kitchen with her reminded him of sitting around the table with his mother, just the two of them talking about the news of the day, or what their plans were, or nothing at all. Ella Tate had a comfortable air, yet one that motivated and inspired, too. She had a knack for being interested in everyone and everything and making the person she was talking to feel like the most important person in the world.

Sebastian drank his milk and wondered which part of him Shaw was most comfortable with — the Harold side or the Ella side. He wondered where, ultimately, the Sebastian side would fall and what Shaw would think of that.

26

THE ENTIRE FIRST FLOOR GLOWED. Every lamp, fixture, and overhead light, which Derek scrambled to find the switch to, was turned on. He wanted no quiet spots, no dim lights or cozy atmosphere. He wanted no doubt that this was about the painting and about the school and nothing more. If Sebastian wanted space, he was going to fill that space with light. The afternoon had been mostly a haze of cleaning and cooking and trying absent-mindedly to get ready for their meeting. Occasionally, he'd wonder how the class was going or if any residue of their encounter remained in his mind. The more he thought, the more depressed he got, concluding that a week's worth of avoidance was the answer he was looking for. Sebastian Tate had changed. They both had changed. But apparently only Derek thought there could be something between them.

He sat in the kitchen, staring at the painting of Shaw Manor, and wondered if it was time to pack away all of his past. The last time they were at the table, they'd reconnected, Derek revealing himself to a person he never thought he'd see again. Even when he was offered the spot at Woodlawn, the notion that Sebastian would be here, would be in Shaw's office, was too uncanny. For the first few days, he walked around this president's house in a daze, tripping over packing boxes and making himself unavailable to various deans. He'd thought long and hard about how to approach Sebastian, how to tell him the truth. Derek sighed, leaning back in his chair and staring up at the ceiling. A previous tenant had seen fit to install copper tile, an authentic Shaker decoration, probably in the hope that it would cast a warm glow about the room. It served only to darken the space and give Derek a warped reflection of his state of mind. He had no idea how he wanted to act when Sebastian arrived.

The professor arrived ten minutes late and five minutes into a sudden thunderstorm. "I was packing my car when I lost track of time. Then the rain hit. Sorry." Only slightly damp, Sebastian apologized as he and his umbrella dripped in the foyer.

Derek stood at arm's length and handed the man a towel from the guest bathroom. "No problem. Why were you packing?"

A scared look flashed on Sebastian's face. "I just have some stuff I want to store at the house."

"Yeah. I've seen your office. It could use a cleaning out."

They stared at each other for a second, letting the implication hang in the air between them. Derek's work since showing up at Woodlawn had been geared toward just that: Sebastian cleaning out his office permanently. Derek shifted his eyes away first.

"Actually, I'm moving things around because I'm moving my summer class to my office," Sebastian said with a tone of barely contained sharpness. "The basement room is good for projecting, but the air downstairs is stifling. In my office, I can at least open the windows."

Derek took back the towel and walked toward the kitchen. "What about the wasps?"

Sebastian flinched. "Ah. Well, I guess I can't expect help from the college there, can I?" He walked past Derek into the kitchen. The cool air between them had little to do with the sudden storm.

Derek took an opportunity to appear helpful. "I'll get on it tomorrow."

"What do you want to show me?" Sebastian stood in the kitchen facing Derek as if waiting for directions. The professor was completely on his guard, and Derek couldn't blame him. He'd pressured him, threatened his job, forced a kiss on him, and embarrassed him in front of his class. He realized that only through coercion did Sebastian show up at his door. This wasn't what Derek wanted. This wasn't the atmosphere he wanted them to exist in. He walked slowly to the corner, fully aware that the uncomfortable situation was entirely his doing.

"You remember this painting of the manor house? The one you gave me?"

Sebastian nodded, making no movement forward. He looked squarely at the canvas and not at Derek.

"After you left–" he paused and tried again. "For the last few days, I've been looking closely at it. I think there was originally a figure painted here, near the gate." Derek laid the painting on the kitchen table. The peaks and valleys of the thick oil paint became obvious under the harsh light. Every light in the kitchen, if possible, was turned toward the table, so the simple image of a brick house turned into a topographical landscape.

Sebastian took a few tentative steps forward. "Where?"

"Where the garden gate is," Derek said, pointing to the spot. "I'd forgotten about that gate, to be honest. We always used to hop the wall. I guess that's why I was looking so closely at it." His voice quickened in an attempt to explain his reasoning and to lighten the atmosphere. If he could turn this meeting from coercive into something work-related, that would satisfy him. He wanted desperately to break this barrier between them. They could at least be coworkers, if not friends —or lovers. "I wonder if that gate is still there."

"It is," Sebastian said, nearing the painting and looking more intently at the spot. "Manny just replaced the locking mechanism because the raccoons learned how to open it."

Derek stared at the professor as he stared at the painting. "What? Manny is still there?"

Sebastian, now even more distracted, answered, "Sure. No way I'd fire Manny." He leaned over the canvas, not paying much attention to the conversation. Derek looked at the top of his head, his mouth hanging open. He felt like little Brian again, running behind this older boy, desperate to be noticed. He leaned forward almost close enough to whisper.

"You don't *live* at Shaw Manor, do you?"

Sebastian bent low over the painting for a moment longer, then snapped upright. In the process, the top of his head met the bottom of Derek's chin, and the two fell back away from the table into separate heaps on the floor. Sebastian groaned, holding the top of his head. Derek crawled over to him, wanting to make sure he was alright. His chin and lip throbbed, but he was more worried about Sebastian. The painting, scattered in the collision, lay face down under the table.

"Hey, you alright?" Derek touched the top of Sebastian's head, checking for blood. All clear, he smoothed down the dark hair and nearly leaned in to kiss his forehead. He stopped easily at the look of horror on Sebastian's face.

"Shit, I'm sorry. I'm sorry," Derek said, backing away.

Sebastian drew close. "Blood," he said, pointing to Derek's face. "You bit your lip."

Derek felt the tickle of blood running down his chin and swallowed hard. Sebastian's face was so close, he could make out the fine lines around his eyes and the small mole near his eyebrow. He remembered noticing it when they were kids. It was during a thunderstorm like today. Sebastian grabbed a tissue from the counter and dabbed at his face. If Derek wanted to understand how much he'd fallen, he'd only have to notice his own reflection in the professor's glasses. He was hopeless.

"I am going to kiss you again," he said, not moving.

Sebastian stopped dabbing at his lip, his eyes flickering up to meet Derek's. His ears turned red, and Derek could sense his breathing increasing with his own. Still, he didn't move.

"I mean it," Derek said.

Sebastian stared back at him and blinked slowly, the flush moving from his ears down his neck.

Derek's arms grew weak, halfway between wanting to reach out to Sebastian or give way and let him fall backwards. He didn't have a chance to choose. Sebastian moved forward on his own, pushing him down.

27

HIS HEAD THROBBED, but seeing the blood on Derek's face made something click in his mind. It wasn't a major injury or even one that wasn't deserved. Sebastian thought he probably should have slugged Derek the moment he saw him, the moment he subconsciously knew it was Brian. He thought of all the hours in the last week he had spent sullen, depressed, and confused. More than anything, he was pissed off that this man, not only threatened his job, but made him feel like a love-struck kid.

"I am going to kiss you," Derek said.

Sebastian held a moment before looking at him. He knew once he locked onto Derek's eyes he'd be done, and he wanted to keep as much control over himself as possible. He didn't like being swept away like this, moving at someone else's pace, but he appreciated it. He appreciated the boldness that Derek showed him and his obvious feelings. Sebastian understood those feelings but never reciprocated.

"I mean it," Derek said.

Sebastian felt the whole length of his spine stiffen as if

pulling from some long cache of resolve. His face felt hot, and his heartbeat seemed to fill the room. He studied Derek's face and let all traces of Brian dissolve. He wanted to truly see the man in front of him and not some memory, not some longing from a nostalgic past. What he saw was just pure desire.

Sebastian stopped caring and pushed him down. He kissed him awkwardly at first, trying to position himself comfortably on top of him. It had been a while since his last "relationship," and being the aggressor had never been in his nature. He wanted to take the decision out of Derek's hands, make him understand that he wanted him just as badly but had no confidence. Anger spurred him on. Anger at Derek for disrupting his life and anger at himself for wanting it. He pulled himself forward, straddling Derek and pinning his shoulders to the floor. He drunk-kissed him, blanking out his mind and focusing only on the feel of his tongue in Derek's mouth, sliding along his.

Derek grabbed his waist and forced him closer, grinding their hips together. He heard a soft grunt escape from under him, and Sebastian pushed down harder into the kiss, pleased that he had broken through Derek's composure. His whole body felt hot and fluid, and he desperately needed to catch his breath, but he knew if he broke free, it would be a long time until he found such confidence again.

Derek's hand slid up his back, cradled his neck for a moment, then grabbed a handful of hair on the back of his head, pulling him away.

"Wait," Derek said. He was out of breath and unfocused.

"No," Sebastian said, leaning into him again. The second kiss was softer, less insistent. He wanted to prove he could be as forceful as Derek and that he couldn't be taken so easily. As Derek kept a tight grip on his hair, his other hand slipped around to the front of his pants. He realized he was straining against his jeans, and as Derek moved his hand back and forth in the space between them, he understood Derek was just as excited as he was. Sebastian released his kiss and leaned back, not sure how much further he was ready to go. His desire slowly cooled into embarrassment. Part of him thought of throwing caution to the wind to prove he wasn't a tease.

"Okay," Derek said, putting a hand on Sebastian's chest. "I read you loud and clear." He leaned forward and hugged him. "I get it," he whispered.

Sebastian relaxed, letting himself be held. The sexual tension cooled into an embrace, and they sat there for a moment, finally able to put their affection into action. Sebastian buried his face in Derek's shoulder, fighting back happy tears and hoping like hell one day he could actually say the words. He looked up, and his eyes flickered over to the canvas lying face down under the table. His mind shifted back to his curiosity about the piece, and he reluctantly pulled away from Derek's embrace.

Derek smiled a crooked smile. "I need to..." He looked past Sebastian into the hallway. Sebastian nodded and slid away, letting him up. His own desire seemed to have cooled on its own, but he blushed with pride at the reaction he'd caused in Derek.

He grabbed the canvas and placed it back on the table, under the overhead lamp. The effect was startling and was one of the things Sebastian loved about oil painting. The swirls and ridges of paint rose like waves in an ocean of color. Each flick of the brush or palette knife caused each bump in texture, and he couldn't help but try to assign value and emotion to each ridge. That Campbell Shaw was the artist of this piece meant Sebastian was all too aware of what emotions could be embodied in each stroke. What worried him was the conflict between the art scholar and the orphan — which one was judging Shaw's work right now? He assumed Derek wanted the first, but Sebastian only felt like the latter.

He felt a light hand on his back. Derek stood next to him, smelling faintly of soap. Sebastian suppressed a smug look and leaned closer. "It's the gate area, right? I think I see what you mean." He pulled a pencil out of his bag. "All along here," he said, pointing to a series of swoops that formed a vague shape. "These strokes seem deliberate." He looked up into Derek's face. He was too close.

"Ah," Sebastian continued, "I mean, you could argue that every stroke is deliberate." He blinked and tried to strangle the twelve-year-old inside him who threatened to giggle every time he uttered the word "stroke."

"I mean the brush strokes." It wasn't just the inner twelve-year-old anymore. A smirk appeared on Derek's face, and Sebastian wasn't sure if he should smack it or kiss it off. He ignored it instead.

"Pareidolia suggests we're just seeing a figure because we're human, and that's what we want to see. Our brains want to discover patterns in the world for survival, mostly, and when a pattern is hard to find, sometimes our brains just make them up." He bent down over the painting again, and Derek moved to the other side of the table.

"The fact that I didn't have to point out that it was a person proves it's not pareidolia, right? I mean, you saw it too."

Sebastian looked closer. The thickness of the paint layer was only obvious in the right light, and he was surprised Derek had found it in the first place. He scanned the rest of the canvas, looking for other telltale signs of revision. There was a small spot in the lower right corner, though this shape was less defined.

"I think it's going to take some time to figure out what's underneath," he said. The heat from before had dissipated into a warm calm. As long as he wasn't looking directly at Derek, he could concentrate, mostly. He was acutely aware of exactly where Derek was the entire time he stared at the canvas. It pleased and annoyed him just the same.

Sebastian shifted the canvas along the table to allow the overhead light to highlight it from a different angle. He sat down, getting closer to the sharp ridges and deep valleys of the paint. He tried to pull together a memory of Shaw painting this particular image, standing outside and working in the late afternoon light, Manny chatting to him from the garden gate.

He looked up and caught Derek staring at him. He swallowed hard and said, "Ah, it wouldn't be Manny standing there, would it?"

Derek furrowed his eyebrows. "I can't see why Shaw would cover him up, though. He's as much a fixture of the place as anything here," he waved his hand at the image.

Sebastian nodded, letting his gaze fall back to the canvas. The large brick face of the manor house took up nearly two-thirds of the image, pushing to the left and sitting just off-center. It was offset enough to be deliberate, breaking open the "rule of thirds" and putting the bulk of the painting in a space that seemed too small for it. It gave the manor a sense of massive scale that, in real life, it didn't possess. The title of "Manor" had been bestowed years ago at the insistence of one of the previous owners' wives. A prestigious title that just got handed down like paper gentry: all title, no land. When Sebastian took control of the house, he started working on the history of the place, beginning with its construction in the mid-18th century. It was a project that went in fits and starts, filling in the lonely hours between semesters when he wasn't teaching an ad hoc course on art history to a bunch of jocks. He snorted, laughing at his situation, his class, and mostly, himself.

"You okay?" Derek asked.

He nodded. The signature in the bottom right-hand corner had a year, but it was caked in dust. "Do you have any cotton swabs? I want to see when he painted this."

"Yeah. But it's on the back, I think. Take a look."

Only the paintings that Shaw sold or gave as gifts had labels on the back. Sebastian was surprised to find one here since this was one of the canvases Shaw hung in his office. He'd been surprised at its placement, right next to the door and within sight of the desk. When Sebastian moved in, he wondered why the two professors occupying the space between him and Shaw had never removed it. Angela told him it was out of deference to Shaw, his work, and his teaching. Sebastian had removed it that night.

28

Sebastian sat on the top landing of the main staircase, the perfect spot to see people filing into the manor while still being hidden. Rarely did people look up the staircase unless an adult was descending it. He felt a little like some precocious kid from those Victorian books his mom made him read, not the sixteen-year-old orphan swallowed up in the big house. The door opened, and he leaned forward to see the college president and his wife arriving. The president had a squirrel-like quality about him: small, excited, and always bustling about. The job of college president seemed exhausting, and Sebastian had no idea why anyone would want to do it.

His opinions were fueled by how Shaw talked about the administration at the school and how out of touch with teaching they seemed to be. While Sebastian didn't understand all the nuances, he felt that anyone choosing to teach at a college must value education at least a little. He felt Shaw was being unfair. This was his natural state, though, finding ways to disagree with Shaw's proclamations any chance he got. Not outwardly or to the extent that they would cause an argument, but enough to try to distance himself from his guardian, even as their relationship was just beginning. Perhaps it was his age, or perhaps it was Shaw's distant kindness, but more than likely, it was the ghost of Harold Tate filling the space between the two men. Sebastian felt that an increasing closeness with Shaw would be a betrayal of his father.

He assumed that most of the guests had arrived and quietly made his way down the stairs. He slid through a side room that served as a formal parlor and entered the kitchen through a side entrance. A tall woman with red hair piled atop her head was barking orders to a group of staff not much older than Sebastian. Two young women placed wine glasses onto trays while their male coworkers shuffled tiny items of food around on their own. One of the woman's assistants bumped into him and mistook him for another waiter. "No, I live here," he replied, though he went unheard and unnoticed. He made his way along the far wall, smelling the delicious food but wishing his stomach not to betray Beverly. There was no way he was eating anything from "this caterer woman," as she'd called her. When Sebastian reached the far end of the kitchen, he knocked on the small oak door in the far corner. Beverly's voice came back, annoyed, "What is it?"

He looked around the door into the dark office. Beverly looked up from her desk, the old-fashioned kind that folded out and had a variety of small compartments for letters, pens, and sundries. She'd been writing a letter when he knocked, and as she realized her visitor was Sebastian and not a member of the catering staff, her annoyance melted away, and she smiled. "Ah, my boy, come in and shut the door. I don't want them to remember I'm here."

He did as he was told and plopped himself down in the

puffy chair that squatted in the corner. Many times, he sat here listening to Beverly's stories and gossip. She always ended the session with an admonition that he brought out the gossip in her and sent him off with a confectionary bribe. He cared more for the cakes than the gossip unless it was about Shaw. For some reason, he wanted to know every detail of the man's life, especially those that highlighted the man's flaws. He settled into the chair and, for the first time, felt that he might be getting too old for these sessions. "They bothering you a lot?" he asked, instinctively knowing how to get Beverly going.

"You don't know the half of it, Seb. Where's this? How do you work this? Honestly," she slammed her pen on the desk. "You'd think 'this caterer woman' had never been around a well-run kitchen before."

Sebastian smiled. "The way she was yelling, I think you're right. You never shout like that."

"Indeed, I don't," Beverly said, nearly shouting just like that. "And I wouldn't need a team of young people to exploit for the service as well." She sighed. "I mean, there's nearly as many staff as there are guests. I can't imagine what this must have cost."

"I think that's the point," Sebastian said, excited to add some gossip of his own. She looked at him with one eyebrow raised. He understood this to mean, "Go on."

"I overheard Shaw talking about the party with someone at the college. He said that having the fundraiser at the manor meant bringing in lots of staff and would make the whole ordeal expensive." He watched her face, holding back the one piece of information that he felt was the most important.

Beverly looked past the boy, as if trying to remember Shaw being this crafty. "He was trying to discourage them from using the house?"

"That's what I thought. I don't know if he forgot I was in the office or didn't care. I was sketching by the window. You know what he said next?"

Beverly locked eyes with the boy, as eager to consume gossip as she was to dish it out. Sebastian continued. "The person on the other end must have asked him something about the house, and Shaw said, 'No, I don't already have staff at the house. I have family at the house. You'll have to bring in people if you want a catered event here.' The conversation ended pretty soon after that."

Sebastian waited for her reaction. Beverly leaned back in her chair, a bit stunned. She turned toward the letter she was writing and crumpled it up, tossing it into the nearby bin. 'Two points,' Sebastian thought. She put her pen back in one of the many drawers and slowly lifted the desk panel and latched it shut. Then she spun her chair to face the window. Sebastian looked over her shoulder, and they both watched Manny and Jim in the garden. They were chatting animatedly near the vegetable patch, the one Beverly had designed and Sebastian helped plant. A good portion of the fresh vegetables they ate came from this patch, and it was a point of pride for the whole staff.

Sebastian sat back in his chair and looked at his hands. Staff was the wrong word for what Beverly, Manny, and Jim were to him. Family had always seemed a more appropriate description. He'd been surprised to hear that Shaw felt the same way. With her back still to him, Beverly reached for a tissue. He could hear a quiet sniffling and decided to wait instead of leaving. Sadness sometimes required solitude, he understood. But what Beverly must be feeling wasn't sadness.

"I'm surprised but grateful." She turned to face the boy, her eyes glistening. "Mr. Shaw has his moments and can be stubborn and difficult, but he's never been cruel and never truly treated any of us like staff. More like helpers, if you can understand the difference." She dabbed at her eyes with the tissue and leaned forward, putting a hand on Sebastian's knee. "I fear that he is a terribly lonely man, Seb. I think he wanted you here in part because of that, but I don't want you to think that's the only reason you're here. Nor do I want you to worry about leaving one day."

She grabbed both of his hands into her own and pulled him forward. "I don't want to see you rattling around this house one day, all alone like him. You get out there and find your life, you hear me? You can always come here, but don't stay. There was a loneliness in both of your parents that only died when they were in the room together. You have no siblings and haven't made friends outside these gates. When you're done with school, you go find the person that kills that lonely part of you. Promise me?"

Sebastian squeezed her red, rough hands and nodded. "I promise."

29

____

Sebastian struggled with his keys and the canvas under his arm. He dropped the key ring and swore loudly, confident that the hallway was empty. As he rounded the corner, he saw Willoughby sitting on the bench outside his office, sipping an iced coffee. The man waved and stood up with a grunt. "Sounds like you're having a hell of a morning already," he said, stepping out of the way so Sebastian could open the door.

"Hold this," he said, handing the wrapped canvas over to the physics professor. "What brings you to campus in the summer and especially to my door?" He held the office door open for Willoughby, who then plopped himself in the guest chair. The buttons on his Hawaiian shirt—this one decorated with pink and green beach umbrellas—strained against his belly. The painting he placed gingerly on the desk.

"I heard a few things and wanted to talk to you about them." He sipped his drink, the ice cubes tinkling in the silence. The men stared at each other for a moment. Sebastian instinctively thought that his fledgling relationship with Derek had made the rumor mill, and he cursed himself for meeting him in the president's house. Campuses are the smallest of towns, someone had told him. He searched the friendly face of Willoughby, who smiled around his straw. It was Carl Willoughby that gave him that crumb of truth, he remembered. All those years ago, when he first started. The air conditioning kicked in loudly and broke the moment.

Sebastian moved behind his desk. "I don't know if I can handle any more bad news. Look at this office," he waved his arm around the unorganized room. "There's a very good chance I'll have to clean this out at Christmas."

"That's what I want to talk to you about," Willoughby said and took a final pull on his iced coffee, filling the silence with the gurgling of a drink gone. "You know Becky, in registration?"

"You know I don't," Sebastian answered, slumping his shoulders. After ten years, he'd neglected all professional relationships outside of those that were necessary for him to teach. Willoughby was the biggest exception. The man had practically bulldozed his way into Sebastian's life from his first day on campus. Something about the professor's perpetual optimism wrapped in reality always made Sebastian see things clearly. It's as if only Willoughby could show him the bigger picture. With that, though, Sebastian glanced at the wrapped canvas and wondered what Willoughby would make of this situation.

"She's taken a shine to me, apparently," Willoughby continued, "and she knows we're friends. She said a chunk of the art department classes were pulled from the fall schedule."

Sebastian straightened up in his chair but didn't answer. Instead, he turned on his office computer and logged in. Willoughby sat silently, letting Sebastian discover the details himself. After a moment, Sebastian slammed his hand on the desk. "Shit! You've got to be kidding me?"

"You see now. Only your classes have been pulled. Not Fennel's. Not Yang's. Just yours. She said she got the request yesterday afternoon."

Sebastian looked from the screen to Willoughby and back, knowing the man had more to offer. In a lot of ways, Willoughby filled the void that Shaw left after he passed away. Part father-figure, part friend, he never mistook the man's gossipy nature as malicious. Willoughby felt information allowed people to make better decisions, and by the look on his face, the physics professor was struggling to make a decision of his own. The man looked down into his lap, opening and closing his hands. Sebastian had never seen him unsure before, and it annoyed him. It annoyed him that one more part of his life was being upturned. He pushed him. "And?"

"Becky said the request came from the President's office."

Sebastian snapped back. "What time?"

"Excuse me?"

"What time? Did she say?"

Willoughby was unsettled. "Well, no. She wouldn't have said what time, only it was yesterday afternoon."

Sebastian traced his steps over the last few days. How long had he been avoiding Derek? Was it long enough for him to get mad and do something like this? Was the call made after Derek crashed his class and before Sebastian came to his house? Maybe it was done in haste, and right now, he's trying to fix the situation. He realized one phone call to Derek would clear this up quickly. He reached for his cell phone, which wasn't there.

"Dammit," he said, looking disheartened at the desk phone. "I left my cell phone...somewhere. How do you use this thing again? Dial 9? Or..."

"Sebastian," Willoughby said, leaning forward with a serious look on his face. He rarely used his full name, and his tone lacked the light quality it usually carried. It made Sebastian put down the receiver and grow concerned. "Seb, do you remember when we first met?"

Sebastian shrugged. "It was during my interview, wasn't it? You were one of the 'students' for my teaching trial."

Willoughby shook his head. "Nope. It was long before that. Up at the manor. You were still in high school, I think." The man laughed and scratched at his salt-and-pepper beard. "Though I can't say it was a typical meeting, more of a physical one. It was a party Shaw hosted."

Sebastian nodded, thinking back to the secret guilt of enjoying one of the caterer's canapes. "Were you there?"

"Only just. I was a new faculty member at the time, and Woodlawn was trying to make its way into the 'hard sciences.' Part of a public-facing re-branding of liberal arts. As a new theoretical physicist, I was a bit of a poster boy." He sat a little straighter, and Sebastian smiled. Willoughby normally presented himself as the bumbling professor, good-natured and a bit bright. Those closest to him understood his true genius lay in the classroom. They also failed to understand his research, operating in a dimension far outside their own. Sebastian often wondered if the "bumbling professor" was a performance to put everyone else at ease.

"At the time, I was a bit of an introvert," Willoughby continued, "So I wasn't as great at parties as I am now." He smiled, spreading his arms wide. "If I recall, I was looking for the bathroom, and you stumbled out of a side door, smack into me, spilling my drink all over my only suit."

Sebastian blushed, remembering the incident and his awkwardness. It had been red wine, and the suit was light in color. Somehow, none of the wine got on his clothes, but Willoughby looked like a murder scene. "That was you?"

The man laughed. "Yeah, I was lankier then. It was before they opened the coffee and bake shop on campus." He patted his belly. "Yup, you did a number on me then. Do you remember what I said?"

Sebastian frowned. "I only remember scrambling for towels and apologizing over and over again. I remember being terrified."

Willoughby laughed again. "Yeah, but I told you. Don't worry. I think you may have done me a favor."

They looked at each other, Willoughby waiting and Sebastian struggling to understand the point he was making.

"Look, Seb, I'll be blunt. Think of this as an opportunity. Maybe it's time for you to go somewhere else. You started here straight out of grad school, took up Shaw's old office, his old classes. Christ, you live in his old house. I'm not disrespecting Shaw, but, son, you just don't seem happy at all."

30

SEBASTIAN LOOKED at the wrapped canvas on his desk and marveled at what it represented. Under the burlap was the house where his family lived: Beverly, Manny, Jim, and even the memory of Shaw. Sometimes, in the spring, when the unused rooms were opened up for airing, he could feel the memory of his mother and father roaming about the place. The canvas also represented Derek and their connection, old and new, and he realized that with him, it might be possible to experience true happiness for the first time in his adult life. It was confusing and frustrating and distracting, but it was happiness, he was forced to admit. He looked up at Willoughby, genuine concern on the older man's face, and realized he had little practice in showing his emotions. No wonder the man was worried.

"I don't know, Seb. Maybe it's a good time for you to spread your wings and stop walking in Shaw's footsteps. I think..."

"I'm not," Sebastian interrupted. "It certainly seems that way. Perhaps I am walking in the physical footsteps, but nothing more." He wondered how long Willoughby had been holding back his concern. Months? Years? He wanted to ease the man's mind without going too far into the current shifts in his own life. That would be for later.

"It would be stupid to not take advantage of the privilege I've been given," Sebastian said. "The house, this position. I understood and tried damn hard not to resent what they meant. Administration thought of me as a continuation of Shaw and, well, that suited a young man looking for work. But I think you can agree that I'm not Shaw. I don't paint like he does, not even when I do paint. I don't teach like him. I don't work like him. I don't look like him," and on this last point, he felt a strange ache in his chest. "I am no more the continuation of Campbell Shaw than those bookcases or this desk chair. We merely occupy the same space."

Sebastian stood up and moved toward the windows overlooking the quad. "Why do you think I agreed to teach art to the lacrosse team?"

Willoughby raised his eyebrows. "I assumed it was a way to bump enrollment in arts courses. That or whimsy?"

Sebastian turned to face him. "Have you ever known me to be whimsical?"

Willoughby pursed his lips. "Nope."

"Exactly," Sebastian pointed. "But that's what this was! I had other reasons, but that kid just badgered me into it, and after a while, I was like, 'What the hell? Why not?'"

He walked over to the small portrait of Shaw that hung near the office door. He addressed it. "You were never whimsical. You took it too seriously."

"It?" Willoughby asked.

"Everything. This summer is when it hit me, Carl. That seriousness was his last gift to me, and I was too stupid to reject it. If it weren't for those boys and Derek, I don't..." He stopped, feeling himself with one foot over the edge of a cliff. While he had no doubt Willoughby would support their relationship, Sebastian wasn't even sure it was a relationship. He stood still, looking into the portrait of his mentor and guardian, and waited for the question. But because Carl Willoughby is a prince among men, he never asked it. Sebastian heard the creak of the chair and turned to see his friend getting ready to leave.

"I'm satisfied," he said. "I was worried about you, but it looks like I can stop." He put a hand on Sebastian's shoulder as he passed him. He leaned close. "I never told you, but that night, after I left with a giant red wine stain on my suit, I walked back to campus alone. When I got to the junior faculty dorm, I met a young woman who took one look at me and laughed herself into tears." He squeezed Sebastian's shoulder. "I ended up marrying her, and until the day she passed, my life was full of joy.

"Follow the whimsy, son."

Sebastian felt as if a huge weight had been lifted off of his chest; at the same time, it filled him with this new feeling. He wiped a tear from his cheek and looked back at the portrait of Shaw. "Okay, let's find out what you were hiding."

31

Derek walked lazily through the quad, keeping the arts building in his periphery. He felt giddy and stupid and thought if the Dean of the Business college were to cross his path, he'd probably lead him in a dance across the lawn.

Sebastian had left early. He let him go with a kiss and a promise to return for dinner. He'd been careful and slow, knowing this relationship was still delicate. Derek felt their feelings finally connected, and he'd watched as Sebastian crossed the campus. He got dressed and checked the small cut on his lip. Easily explained, he thought, and started humming something from long ago. Something his mother sang when she was happy.

As he neared the administration offices, his phone buzzed, and he juggled his coffee to answer it, hoping it was Seb.

"President Morton," said a woman's voice. "It's Madeline in the Registrar's office. Would you have some time today to go over your changes?"

Derek slowed his stride. "I'm heading that way now for a meeting, so I'll pop in." He hung up without saying goodbye.

The morning sun felt nice, but the air seemed thicker than usual. It was going to be a sticky one. He quickened his pace, wanting to duck into the air-conditioned building when he stopped. He looked down at his phone. What changes?

"ALL OF THESE requests came from me, you say?" Derek stared over Madeline's shoulder at her computer monitor. A spreadsheet listing the fall offerings at Woodlawn showed each class categorized by their respective colleges—College of Arts and Sciences, College of Business, etc. She pointed to the large blocks of yellow containing classes currently being removed from the schedule per the president's request. Derek scanned the list, reaching past Madeline to scroll with the mouse. The woman rolled her chair out of the way, giving him room.

There were a lot of classes highlighted in the College of Arts and Sciences. More classes were cut than he would have even considered when working on the new, leaner offerings. He scanned the professor names and saw three of Sebastian's classes were on the chopping block. How did this happen? Derek scrolled past the art classes but barely registered what others were in danger. He'd been planning on phasing things out gradually. And now, after...well, he certainly wasn't going to just eliminate all of Seb's classes.

He turned to the registrar. "From me? You're sure?"

She nodded. "I thought the request was a bit much, so I asked IT to verify the user ID of the request. They said it was yours."

"But I didn't put in any requests for cancellations. I wouldn't do that this close to the fall semester. Current students already have their schedules, and the few new students we have will think there was a bait and switch if we change the catalog now."

Madeline nodded, the stern face she'd met Derek with when he walked into the office softening. "That's what I thought as well." She stood and looked over the top edge of her cubicle. "Didn't I say it was weird, Becky?"

A woman's voice called back. "You sure did, Maddy."

"See?"

Derek stood up and scratched the back of his head. He turned to Madeline and could see her eyes flick up from the cut on his lip. He smiled. "Bit my lip in my sleep, I think."

"You're not having the best day, are you?" Madeline asked. 'I was,' he thought, then said, "You haven't actually canceled these classes, right?"

"Nope. I'm guessing they're staying for now?"

"Absolutely," Derek said and looked past Madeline to the woman peeking her head above her cubicle. She had salt-and-pepper hair and thick eyebrows. He guessed this was Becky and that she was looking for assurances. "No cancellations," he said, directing it at her.

Becky nodded her head once and ducked back down behind the beige felt.

Derek asked Madeline for her contact in the IT department before thanking the women and heading to his appointment. The morning had crashed so quickly, and over something so confusing, that he worried the night before had been a dream. The pain from the coffee cup hitting his lip was enough assurance.

He greeted a few people in the stairwell and made his way up to the Deans' offices. He needed to make changes but wanted to discuss with each department individually how best to do it. He certainly wouldn't have cut most of Seb's, certainly not now. Even if Seb hated him, he'd never be that vengeful.

Derek stopped three steps from the third floor, his stomach turning. He hoped like hell this hadn't gotten around campus already. Rumors flew across the quad faster than a blue jay in spring. He pulled out his phone to call Seb, knowing that being completely honest about the situation would be best.

The third-floor door swung open, and the Dean of Business stepped onto the landing. "Hello there, Derek," he called. "I'm glad I caught you."

Derek pocketed his phone and took the last few steps toward the dean. His call would have to wait.

32

SEBASTIAN SURPRISED himself with his restraint in hanging
up the phone. He wanted to slam the receiver through the top
of his desk, but in the last second, he pulled back. Taking a few
deep breaths, he thought about his next move. He scanned the
still messy office and took in the piles of books and tilting
stacks of articles and papers. He normally felt calm and safe in
here, his hermit's hut on the edge of campus. He noticed the
painting he'd brought from Derek's the night before. It leaned
against the closest bookcase, the red of the manor glaring at
him through the dim light of the room. Sebastian's calm left
him instantly.

He kicked out a pile of library books and felt a twinge of
guilt. Yet, he raged on, shoving his office chair into the wall and
grunting out an expletive each time he came into contact with
something he could kick or hit. 'How could they eliminate his
entire semester,' he thought. 'Without even contacting me?'
He stopped to look out the west window toward the big house
across the quad. No lights shone in the windows, so its occupant must be out. Why didn't he say anything?

Sebastian slammed his foot into the baseboard and immediately regretted it. Pain throbbed in his pinky toe, and he hobbled back to the guest chair near the door. He remembered sitting in this chair the first time Shaw brought him to campus. It was a month after his parents had died, and Beverly had convinced Shaw to get the boy out of the house for a bit. The chair held the same soft richness that he felt for the first time, cradling his body, small then, less small now. The memory only made him angrier.

Running his hands along the leather upholstery, he thought about his conversation with Willoughby, how only yesterday his assurances seemed real. He'd believed that confidence, but that word "footsteps" lingered. He chilled sitting in the chair, Shaw's chair, not his. It was his office now, but it had been Shaw's. Most of these books had been his. The desk, the window shades, at least half of the bookcases, even the wasps are part of Shaw's legacy. He'd been here first. He'll always have been the first, Sebastian thought. Everything in his life was connected to the great Campbell Shaw, and Sebastian was about to lose it all.

The red brick in the manor painting caught Sebastian's gaze, and he glared at it. At this distance, the obvious cover-up near the gate was invisible; only the massive bulk of the building was clear. He felt the presence of that place, and by extension, Campbell Shaw himself. Even the people he called his friends, Beverly, Manny, Jim, even Willoughby, had all been Shaw's first. 'Nothing but hand-me-downs here,' he thought. I've been a rotten caretaker.

Without classes to teach in the fall, Sebastian would be stuck doing administration work, preparing for the dismantling of the department. He still had art majors to advise through their final years, but he'd have to focus on his own scholarship and the search for a new position. Since he'd abandoned his research work completely after achieving tenure, he realized that the job search would take priority. He glowered, slumping deeper into the chair. He'd only gotten the position at Woodlawn because of his connection with Shaw. They'd seen him as a continuation of the great man and his work. When they realized they'd only hired a sullen art historian instead of a charismatic artist, well, by then it was too late, and Shaw was long dead.

He stared at the painting, letting the brick red seep into his brain and mood. He'd achieved nothing of his own and, even now, the only interesting things in his life had been given to him by Shaw: this painting and Derek. He sighed. "I'd like to return both, right now," he said, standing then walking over to the canvas.

Sebastian stared down, his head hanging at a slight tilt, letting the painting blur into his vision until it was just splotches of red, green, and gray. Despair gave way to anger again, and he imagined himself without a Campbell Shaw in his life. It was empty. No, not exactly. It was just devoid of Shaw. He couldn't see the other side of his imagination. Shaw's presence loomed as large as his absence. He focused his eyes on the canvas, taking in the details of each brick and stone. He pictured himself plucking them from the picture and smashing each and every window.

Tears dripped onto his cheek as Sebastian kicked hard at the painting, an original Campbell Shaw. He kicked over and over again. The ash backboard prevented his foot from going clean through the canvas. Flakes of green paint covered the top of his sneakers. He'd kicked into the stacked paint near the iron gate. Something yellow peeked out from behind the green.

There was a quick knock on his office door, and before he

could say "go away," Casey and two of his teammates slid into the room. Sebastian's anger shifted to confusion, and then the automatic Rolodex in his head started spinning as he tried to remember the other students' names. It usually took him into the fifth week of a semester to get half of his students' names straight.

Casey was easy to remember because he was bright, cheerful, and a damn nuisance. The boy to his left, pale and ginger, appeared to have just woken up. He seemed the least eager to take these summer lessons but acted out of loyalty to his team captain. Sebastian thought his name might be Brock.

The other one could have been Sebastian's more handsome and likable brother, and that annoyed him instantly. He'd always counted on his dark countenance to keep people at bay, and here was this younger version of himself having the time of his life. This one was definitely Riley.

Sebastian tried not to sneer. "What?"

Casey squinted and took a step toward Sebastian. "You okay, Dr. Tate?"

He suddenly remembered the tears of frustration. He took a deep breath but didn't wipe his face. "We have class today?"

Possibly Brock said, "We were going to just study, but the room downstairs is closed. The IT guy is replacing the projector, and they have the whole ceiling down. Probably just trying to do more than necessary."

Casey laughed. "Brett's dad is a contractor, which makes him suspicious. We thought we could study up here with you?"

Who the hell is Brett? Sebastian thought, then updated Brock to Brett in his mind's Rolodex.

"No," he said and turned from them. He walked around to the back of his desk, pulled his chair from under the window, and sat down. "I'll see you next time."

"But," Casey said, approaching. "You said we were going to have a test soon, and I thought it would be a good idea..." Riley put a hand on his captain's shoulder. Casey stopped and glanced at him. The other boy just shook his head.

"I'm not in the mood right now, so go." Sebastian looked at the phone on his desk, seeing and not seeing at the same time.

"But Dr. Tate, we..."

"Get the hell out of my office." With each word, Sebastian raised his voice a bit more until he was practically yelling. He regretted it the moment it came out of his mouth, but right now, when he felt at his absolute worst, these students, these kids with their futures and their youth, were suffocating him.

Brett, not Brock, took a step forward, but Casey held up his hand. "Got it," he said. He nodded once and turned to leave. Riley followed without a glance. Brett held back for a moment, looking at Sebastian. When he finally turned away, his gaze fell on the painting of Shaw Manor.

Brett stopped and pointed at the canvas. "Looks like a cover-up there."

Sebastian followed the boy's gaze to see the buckled bits of paint. When he turned to ask Brett what he meant, he had gone.

33

DEREK WALKED out the side entrance to the administration building and into a bright day. He picked the heavy metal door since it gave him good cover when he decided to slam it in anger. The loud bang echoed in the small parking area near the brick building, and he looked around sheepishly, ready to offer his sincere apologies. *I just don't know my own strength, ha ha,* he planned to say. But as he strode off toward his next errand, he found himself unbothered.

He stepped into one of the well-worn paths that crisscrossed the central quad on campus. Years ago, the trustees had tried to convince staff that letting students cut across the lawn was "uncouth" and "rebellious." Derek pulled out his phone and pressed Sebastian's contact listing. The call, again, went to voicemail, and he swore under his breath. Again, he looked to see if he'd been caught, the young president unable to handle the stress of the job, muttering to himself in the middle of campus. He crossed into the central plaza of the quad and stopped. Two men were flipping over the cement benches that lined the concrete area. One of them noticed Derek, winked, and then went back to ignoring him. He was about to ask the men what they were doing when he noticed the campus maintenance truck parked just across the lawn. Derek left the men alone and continued across campus.

He didn't know if it was the sun or his anger that forced the sweat onto his brow. Wiping his face with the back of his forearm, he thought of Manny, working out in the gardens of Shaw Manor. The big man liked to wink at the boys when they snuck around the grounds. Manny always seemed two steps ahead of the two. He and Sebastian would take the slowest, most silent steps two young boys could make, only to turn a corner and see that red, winking face smiling at them. Manny would hold a finger up to his lips and then surreptitiously point to Jimmy, leaning against a tree, or one time, napping in a wheelbarrow. Jimmy was an easy target for the boys' pranks, and Brian wondered if he'd always been in on the joke.

He reached the other side of the vast lawn and smiled. Those days at Shaw Manor were always filled with adventure. Derek reached the computer department's offices, stopping just outside the door. He thought about his luck in reuniting with Sebastian after all these years. He tried Sebastian's phone again. No answer. The thought of a stupid mistake ruining it after all this time brought his anger back to the surface. *It better damn well be a mistake*, he thought, and softly opened the office door.

"KELLEY MCPHERSON IS WHO YOU WANT," the student at the desk said, barely looking up from his laptop. He pointed a thumb over his shoulder, giving Derek the direction of the person in question. "Server room."

Derek grunted out a "thanks" and walked down a short hallway toward the wide, windowed room at the far end. A small bell jingled as he entered, and as the door closed behind him, Derek shivered in the chilly air of the server room. The background hum of the heavy-duty air conditioner made him feel like he'd entered a working beehive, and his arms broke out into gooseflesh.

"Hello?" he called out. Only a laptop on the workstation before the racks of blade servers suggested someone was on duty. Small green and red lights peeked through snakes of cables, joining each of the servers into a mysterious network that somehow helped Woodlawn chug along. He felt the cool air rise from the floor vents and wished he'd worn closer-fitting pants.

From behind a cart of old computer monitors emerged a man in his fifties, wearing a T-shirt and cargo shorts, carrying a hoagie. He spotted Derek shivering by the entrance and waved his lunch in greeting. "Ah, El Presidente," the man said. "Madeline called to let me know you were on your way. Come on back to the cockpit."

Kelley McPherson turned away and led Derek into a small office near the back of the room. Here, the walls were of the cinder block variety that most of the mid-1980s buildings on campus sported. Aside from the pristine desktop, the small dark office was stuffed with what looked to Derek like old computer manuals, pamphlets, and handmade zines. There was no obvious place for him to sit down, so he hovered near a stack of folders labeled "Replacement Logs" and enjoyed the break from the air and noise of the server room.

Kelley sat down at his desk and let Derek remain standing. "I took the time to go through our logs in case you stopped by today." He spun in his chair and placed his wrapped hoagie carefully on a stack of old Wired magazines on the shelf behind him. "Madeline knows her stuff when it comes to the registration system, so she had the timestamps ready to go. She's one of the good ones," he said, eyeing Derek to see if he was going to turn out to be one of the good ones, too.

"She helped me out a lot today," he said. "I hope you can solve the mystery." He extended the President Smile, but it felt forced and, more importantly, he thought Kelley could see right through it. Derek sighed.

"It's all a mess," he added, dropping the pretense. "I wouldn't have made any changes without faculty approval."

The IT director seemed to measure Derek up and weigh both responses: the smile and the concern. Seeming to decide, he pursed his lips and clapped his hands. "I got you, El Presidente. I got you."

Derek leaned over the man's shoulder as he brought the monitor to life and realized he'd received his first campus nickname. *Not the worst*, he thought and then squinted at the dizzying list of green numbers filling the black screen.

Kelley pointed to a grouping of entries, all with a time stamp of 03:50. "Early this morning, 'you' logged into the registration system and made a bunch of changes. Here," he slid his finger down the list. "Here and here, too."

Kelley hit the Print Screen button, and somewhere in the distance, a small engine whirred. "I can't see exactly what changes were made, mind you—that's what Madeline showed you—but we can match our log times here with her database changes there and have some pretty good circumstantial evidence.

He rose and crossed the room, returning with a clipboard. "I have a list of all the IP addresses registered on campus. The students have generalized ones through the Wi-Fi and their individual ISP and phone accounts, but all the admin and faculty offices are individualized." He flipped through the pages, each one containing more numbers, similar to those on the screen. Each number seemed to correspond with a building name.

Kelley stopped shuffling. "Ah, there's the one." He pointed to the entry logs on the screen and then matched it with the page he'd flipped to. "I can give you the building and office, but that's about it." He tilted the clipboard so Derek could see where he pointed.

"You know this one?"

Derek felt the chill of the server room penetrate his skin. His face felt hot, and he unconsciously flexed his hands. "Yes. Yes, I know this one."

He'd known from the moment he'd heard about the canceled classes. Of course, he'd known.

Derek held out his hand. "Thank you. I'll remember this when you hand in your budget for next year."

Kelley laughed. "You're one of the good ones, too, I see."

Derek smiled and turned toward the door. 'Not for long,' he thought. 'Not for long.'

34

SEBASTIAN, *18 years old*

Sebastian tripped over the final steps, the large suitcase unbalancing his already awkward gait. The last year of high school had not been kind to the late bloomer, and it seemed that he'd sprouted in all manner of ways over the summer. Beverly gasped, surprised by the noise, then shuffled over to him. "What are you doing?" she said, pointing at the luggage. "You should get Jimmy to bring that down."

Sebastian scowled and dropped the bag more heavily than necessary. "I'm perfectly capable of carrying my luggage," he said. He swiped his overgrown hair away from his face. "What's in there?" He saw the small cooler sitting atop the few boxes of books he'd packed for the trip to Boston.

She smiled. "I packed some of your favorites for the ride, including those double-chocolate brownies you tell me always keep you awake at night." She patted him lightly on his arm. "Can't have you falling asleep behind the wheel."

He gave her an annoyed look but felt grateful. The worst part about attending university away from home was leaving

Beverly's cooking behind. He couldn't imagine anything at Boston U tasting half as good. Sebastian noticed her wringing hands held tight to her chest. He knew she was worried about his leaving for the semester, but he felt there was something else troubling her.

"What's wrong?"

She tilted her head and whispered, "He wants to talk to you one more time."

Sebastian sighed. "There's nothing more to say," he said. He pulled the car keys out of his pocket, letting them jingle at his side. If Shaw was listening, that should have given him a clue that he was ready to leave.

"Seb, just go talk to him. You're not going to see him until winter break." She put a hand on his back and pushed him gently toward the door. It was already ajar as if anticipating his entrance. "Go," she whispered and shoved him forward.

Campbell Shaw sat on the edge of his large mahogany desk, waiting for him. When Sebastian stumbled in, the old man slowly rose to his feet and smiled. The years had taken most of the vigor out of the artist. The manor had felt empty in the last couple of years as the number of college events hosted by Shaw dropped off. Sebastian knew the man wanted to retire, and the trustees kept convincing him to stay. He also knew that there was another reason Shaw wanted to keep teaching.

"I know you're about to head out," he said, holding out his hand. "I just wanted to plead my case one last time."

Sebastian shook his head at the offered hand. "I'm already enrolled at Boston, sir. I think it's the best option for me. We've talked this out already."

"I know, I know," Shaw said, moving toward the unlit fireplace. He touched a photo on the mantel, the one of Sebastian and his parents during their first stay in the manor. "I had hoped that you could be one of my students."

Sebastian watched him and wondered if touching the picture was to invoke the memory of his mother and father. The obligation Shaw had made to the young orphan all those years ago hung quietly between the two. His decision not to attend Woodlawn had cut Shaw pretty deep, but he had to understand that Sebastian needed to break away. As he watched the old man by the fireplace, he had a sudden flash of memory, of standing just outside the door to this room, peeking in and seeing someone else standing there. His face flushed, and he grew uneasy.

"Wasn't I student enough here at home?" he asked, trying to shake the old image from his mind.

"I don't think you ever got the best of me as a teacher," Shaw replied. "I think you'd thrive at Woodlawn, and I'd be able to give you guidance." He paused before adding. "Your father would have wanted you to follow in his footsteps."

Sebastian felt a stab of pain in his stomach. "My father had talent as an artist. If he were still alive, he'd agree with me."

"Your father wasn't nearly as talented as I thought," Shaw said. A light flashed in the man's eyes that startled Sebastian, and he realized he'd touched on a sore spot in Shaw's memory.

"If my father had no talent, why did you make us stay here?" Sebastian parried. The flush at the fading memory turned to anger, and he felt he needed to stick up for his father, if not himself. "Why did you keep insisting the whole family come here so he could paint?"

The image of a woman standing before the fireplace, a woman with a pleading look on her face, flared up in his mind. At first, the woman had the face of his mother, but before he could realize the error, it changed. Brian's mother stood there, just as she had that night years ago. The shame of the moment and the anger at Shaw's insult twirled into each other. His stomach felt sour, and his mouth worked on its own. "Or," he spat out, "was it Mom you really wanted here?"

Shaw leaned backwards, his shoulders hitting the molding of the fireplace, the force of the statement knocking him back. "What nonsense are you saying?"

"Maybe that's why we were always here, right?" Sebastian took a few steps forward, liking the feeling of having the upper hand, finally, in this relationship. He wasn't an artist, he knew, but he also knew that his father had plenty of talent. How many paintings did he see his father work on while he and Brian gallivanted around the place? How many landscapes did his mother show off every time someone would come to visit? Sebastian took one more step forward, thinking that of all the pictures hanging in this empty, soulless house, not a damn one had been painted by his father. "Was my mother your real target?" He said, shouting now. "Were you after her, just like Brian's mom?"

Shaw's face contorted with rage, and a flush blotched his neck and cheeks. He sputtered and stammered and barely got out the words "that was different. She had-"

"You ran them out of here when Brian went missing. Then you got rid of my parents and were stuck with me." Sebastian caught his breath and realized he was heading toward the point of no return. He decided to plunge in headfirst.

"Your guilt made you take me in, and you tried to make me in your own image. Well," and again, he took a step forward. The old man had nowhere left to turn, and he could see Shaw wincing as if he was about to be slugged. "What a damn disappointment we both are, right?"

They stood there, watching each other, tension neither

rising nor falling but present as the brick wall that lined the gardens outside. Neither spoke until the sound of Sebastian's car could be heard coming around the driveway. Someone had brought it up front for his drive to school. He took that as a sign and turned away from Shaw, who didn't stop him.

Out in the hallway, Beverly tried to stop him, but he brushed past her and grabbed his suitcase.

"Yo, Seb. I put the boxes in the back for ya," Jim said, tossing him the car keys. "You drive safe."

Sebastian nodded, stopping in the doorway. To Beverly, he said, "Thank you. I'll see you soon."

He nodded once at Jimmy, then turned to see Shaw in the doorway to the den. The man looked small, old, no longer the oversized presence in Sebastian's life. No longer the man he had to live up to.

Sebastian said nothing and left. He didn't return for another four years.

35

SEBASTIAN RETURNED TO HIS OFFICE, carrying a small set of painting tools and a can of paint thinner. The set he'd found in one of the older art rooms, one that had been unused for the spring semester. He unrolled the canvas wrap, uncovering three small brushes, a palette knife, and two long, thin picks with carved wooden handles. From his pocket, he brought out a small ceramic saucer and placed it on his desk near the brushes. He poured a small amount of thinner into the saucer, and his office filled with the acrid smell.

He walked behind his desk, looked left and right for any wasps, and cracked the window. If he didn't get some air soon, he thought he'd pass out.

The manor painting sat where he'd left it, leaning against the bookcase. Bending over it for a moment, Sebastian tried to remember Shaw painting this piece. He was known for his landscapes and occasional architecture studies, but Sebastian couldn't remember Shaw setting up outside in the gravel driveway to paint his own house. It felt so unlike the man he remembered. So utterly domestic. If there was one thing Sebastian knew about Campbell Shaw, it was his lack of senti-mentality.

With a grunt, he hefted the canvas up and onto his desk. He pulled the desk light close, focusing the light on the area by the iron gate. Brett, not Brock, knew his stuff, Sebastian thought and picked a bit at the globs of vermilion and green with his fingernail. Nothing but a white blotch behind the lumps of paint could be seen, and, for all he knew, it was just the original canvas. Sebastian dipped the smallest brush into the thinner and leaned in. It had been quite some time since he last did any restoration work—sometime during his masters, he thought. It was delicate and deliberate work, and he knew he was in for a long afternoon.

After five minutes, Sebastian tossed the last paintbrush into the trash can and swore. 'This is getting me nowhere,' he thought and leaned up to check his progress. Nothing seemed to have changed, even with switching to the larger brushes. He started working on the flakes of paint near the edge of the expo-sure, thinking he could just work on widening the spot, but it was no use. Whatever paint Shaw decided to use that day was not intimidated by decades-old paint thinner and an inexperi-enced restorer. He looked over the rest of his tools and reached for the thinner of the two picks, then stopped. The words "that's a cover-up job" came flowing into his ears again.

He bent low over the spot again. This canvas had been unceremoniously stacked along with several other unremark-able Shaw paintings of the campus buildings. They were pass-able, but practice studies, their value only in their history and not their artistic flair. It had also been wrapped in a loose canvas covered with burn marks. Sebastian's eyes traced over the smoother strokes on the rest of the painting and the simple cherry frame with a cove molding. Looking closely now, he could see darker spots around the edges of the frame, faint through the stain. This, too, is a cover-up, he thought and ran his hand over the wood.

Staring at the painting, he could feel the pressure of the office around him. The desk had been Shaw's, the chair, the phone, the window shades, even the threadbare rug in the corner, all picked out at one time by his predecessor. Sebastian kept it a mess, stumbling over piles of books and towers of ungraded papers threatening to suffocate him, in part because he couldn't bear to see the space as neat and organized as it had been during Shaw's time but mostly in an attempt to make it his own. In his failure—or more, lack of desire—to become a practicing artist in his own right, he had no idea how to distinguish himself from the presence of his mentor.

He seemed to lean closer to the swirls of yellow and green, the odor from the traces of paint thinner filling his nose. His eyes watered, and his head felt light. Part of his mind warned him he was heading face-first into the canvas. Another part thought if he concentrated, he'd fall face-first into the past. He blinked and slid his gaze to the bottom right corner of the painting, where Shaw normally put his signature. Sebastian furrowed his brow and read: "CS 1993."

The man always signed his full name, but this one carried only his initials. It was definitely a Shaw painting. He could tell by the idiosyncratic way he painted light on the foliage and foreground areas. Yet, something about this piece felt personal. Then, Sebastian realized that this had been a gift.

"Who's gift?" he muttered.

Certainly not for him, he thought, and the anger from earlier returned, building up steam until he reached out for the palette knife and deliberately plunged it into the mass of paint. Sebastian stabbed and dug, ripping up layer after layer as if roughly weeding the ivy and vines represented in the image. He cut through wads of verdant green, revealing a lighter yellow and lime pattern underneath. His stomach clenched, and, thinking it was a reaction to his destruction of the canvas, Sebastian sniffed and plunged in again, ripping more and more away. He accidentally dug too deep into the canvas, and he held back, holding the palette knife just above a clump of green. The paint blob was partially detached, and, holding his breath, he slowly flicked the full splotch off. It landed just outside the frame on the desktop, but Sebastian didn't watch where it fell.

He stared at the small, pink face of a baby cradled in a woman's arms. Squinting, he realized the yellow and lime pattern filled the top half of her body, a recognizable sweater with gold buttons. Her hair was golden, and her face was tilted down toward her child. Sebastian held his hand out, nearly touching the face of a young mother, Jenny, looking lovingly down at her infant son, Brian.

What the hell is he doing here? He looked at C.S. in the bottom right corner and back at the imposing facade of Shaw Manor. A Manor had permanence and history. A Manor took up space in a community in ways that other homes did not. A Manor was passed down through families like a title. Sebastian looked at the image of Jenny and Brian.

A Manor was passed from father to son.

"So that's why you came back," he said to the empty room.

The office phone rang, but he knocked it off his desk in his haste. He grabbed the painting and stormed out of the door, the faint scent of paint thinner trailing behind.

36

SEBASTIAN, *22 years old*

Sebastian stood near the iron gate, watching the cars rumble in and out of the manor driveway. Manny did his best to control the flow of traffic, but the sheer number of mourners made those anxious to pay their respects, or at least be seen doing so, park up and down the avenue. Groups in black and gray passed in and out of the main entrance, chatting, laughing, and a few even caring enough to cry. Sebastian kept out of their line of sight and tried to dissolve into the background. Had he been able, he would have escaped into the gardens, but Manny had the sense to padlock the gate, not wanting the "lookie-loos" trampling all over his hard work.

Sebastian had only returned that morning and had spent the last few days apologizing to a tearful Beverly over the phone. He'd been in the middle of his senior thesis, and his adviser, though a fan of Shaw's work, wouldn't give Sebastian the time to help with the arrangements. "You're not family," he said dismissively. "Go back after your presentation." Sebastian ghost-walked through his whole thesis, barely passing.

He leaned against the low brick wall, the base of the main wrought-iron fence. Thick English ivy crowned his head as he tilted it back. Goosebumps broke out on his neck as he touched the cold bars. They felt impenetrable, and he wondered, for the first time, why Shaw Manor had been built like a fortress. For almost four years, Sebastian had lived on the other side of those iron bars. Manny's padlock suggested that he was on this side for good.

"Seb," Manny called to him. A middle-aged woman with blond hair stood next to the groundskeeper. She followed Manny's gaze and found Sebastian beside the wall. Their eyes met for a moment, and then the woman shook her head and hurried to the front door. Sebastian watched as he shuffled over, unconcerned but feeling something tug at a forgotten memory.

"Who was that?" he asked.

Manny waved a Lincoln Town Car through. "Not sure, to be honest. She asked if you were here, though."

Sebastian turned toward the front door, but the woman had disappeared in a sea of mourning suits.

"Maybe one of Shaw's friends," he said and shrugged. "They all probably think I'm still his little orphan." He stared at his feet and at the sneakers he had worn home that morning. When Beverly took hold of him as he stepped out of his car, she rushed him upstairs to change. Bustling about him, switching between sobbing into her sleeve and hugging Sebastian tightly, she'd discovered his missing dress shoes and offered a pair of Shaw's. He emphatically declined. The symbolism would have been more than he could bear.

They stood outside for a while, Manny controlling the traffic and Sebastian watching but thinking of nothing. When the flow of mourners slowed to a trickle, Manny checked his watch and declared, "I think that's it for the latecomers. Hernando!" He called out to a young man directing cars at the exit.

"Take over for me, okay?"

"Got it." The young man looked Sebastian up and down. He felt strangely inspected and flushed under the gaze. "Sorry for your loss," he added, then turned away.

"Yeah. Thank you." Sebastian hung his head, not wanting to meet the young man's gaze. He'd never met him before, but something made him uneasy. Manny's hand on his shoulder gave him a start.

"Let's go inside."

He led Sebastian back to the iron gate and unlocked the chain. The two men slipped inside, Manny returning the lock to its place. The path looked the same as Sebastian remembered, with clover covering and Hosta plants surrounding the remains of an old stone stable. There had been at least two attempts at reconstructing the building during Sebastian's time living at Shaw Manor, but both ended in a muddy mess. Manny had warned Shaw that the ground around the ruins held about as much as it could, and it was best to let it be. It took two frustrated contractors and thousands of dollars before he realized Manny was right.

Snaking away from the driveway and under the cover of black walnut trees, the path offered cover from the noise in front and inside the house. The men walked in silence, and Sebastian counted the paving stones as he stepped on each one. He stifled the urge to hop from one to another, as he did so many times when he was younger. Always alone, he thought. Then, the blonde woman's face flashed in his mind. No, not always alone.

Before he could grab the thread of that memory, Jimmy

came bounding around the corner. "Found you," he said to Sebastian, then turned to Manny. "I've been kicked out of the kitchen again."

"No surprise," Manny said, smiling. "Look at you!"

In the short time before the memorial, Sebastian got to catch up a bit with Manny and Jimmy, the two men who seemed to loom nearly as large in his life as Campbell Shaw. While Manny seemed to only have added a bit of gray at his temples, Jimmy had taken on quite a bit of girth around his center. At Sebastian's surprised face, he said, "Oh. I got married to a great cook last year, and, well, she spoils me." He patted his ample tummy and grinned. Life had continued at Shaw Manor after he left, Sebastian knew, but he was startled by how much he suddenly regretted leaving.

"Anyway," Jimmy said, leading the men around the side of the house. "Lawyer wants you. Bigby. He's smoking on the deck." He pointed past the corner of the brick wall toward the garden deck. The tall, bald Bigby stood primly, holding a cigarette with his back to the house. His left arm was held firmly in place behind his back, and Sebastian could see the top of a briefcase sitting at his feet. He looked like a man waiting for orders.

Anxiety welled up inside his chest, and he wanted nothing more but to run away.

Jimmy patted him on the arm. "Go on. Finish the business, then come to the kitchen. Beverly wants you with her."

Jimmy's eyes were a deep brown and seemed overwhelming at that moment. Since he'd returned to the manor, he'd felt cold and out of place, like an alien. But one soft look from Jimmy Maldonado, and he was home again.

Sebastian walked toward the lawyer without a look back.

He knew that one glance from Manny's kind, red face would break him on the spot.

SEBASTIAN STEPPED QUIETLY onto the deck, and the man turned. Though he had nearly six inches on Sebastian, Bigby the Lawyer, as he thought of him now, slouched a bit when he saw the young man approach. He smiled softly, small wrinkles appearing on his face as he did, and Sebastian was immediately put at ease. While he knew what the presence of the lawyer meant, this man didn't seem to mean him any harm.

"I have heard much about you, Mr. Tate. You are as Mr. Shaw described you." He deftly shifted his cigarette and held out his hand for Sebastian. The sweet smell of cloves drifted between them, and this was the first time he could remember not coughing in the presence of a cigarette.

"Thank you, I think," Sebastian said. They shook hands quickly and let go.

The kitchen door opened briefly, and the sounds of curt directions to the catering staff trickled out into the yard. Both men turned toward the building, but whoever had opened the door retreated back into the house.

"There are guests that will be curious about our meeting," Bigby said, drawing Sebastian's attention back to him. The tall man bent neatly at the waist and put out his cigarette on the concrete. Still bent, he pulled a small pouch from an inner breast pocket and stuffed the cigarette butt inside. As he straightened, he pulled a folder out of his open satchel. "This is an informal meeting. I will need you to come to the office at a later date." Bigby opened the folder and cleared his throat.

"To Sebastian Tate, my ward, I leave the entirety of Shaw

Manor. The endowment that supports it shall continue under the supervision of Hanover Bigby until Sebastian Tate takes up permanent residence in the Manor or decides to abdicate his ownership and responsibility." He closed the folder with a snap. "There are a lot more stipulations and caveats, but you get the idea."

Sebastian stared at the closed folder in Bigby's hands. He'd never seen a man's hands so clean and manicured. He was used to Manny and Jimmy's rough, dirt-encrusted hands or Shaw's gnarled fingers almost always smeared with ink or paint. He looked down at his own hands, those unable to recreate the talents of his father and Shaw. His hands seemed able to only hold books about art, not produce it. The small, callous bulging on the top of the right hand's middle finger suggested the hands of a writer, not an artist. These hands haven't been in the ground in years, he thought. What could these hands do with all this?

"I will leave you to the rest of the gathering," Bigby said, picking up his satchel and holding out his hand again. "Beverly has my contact information. Please don't hesitate to call with any questions. Can you come to my office at the beginning of next week?"

Sebastian looked up into the man's face, expecting business and seeing only kindness. Tears welled up in his eyes for the first time since he'd been back. Shaw is really gone, he thought. Campbell Shaw was gone and left him everything. The whole thing felt uneasy and dreamlike, but it wasn't a dream. The lawyer was proof of that.

His voice cracked. "Yeah, that's fine." Sebastian hung his head and tried to hold back his sobs. He immediately failed.

Bigby patted his shoulder as he walked away. "My condolences, Mr. Tate. Sincerely."

37

Derek slammed the front door and winced. He turned and reminded himself that the semester was over; there would be few people who would have seen his behavior. Still, with his presidency in the honeymoon phase, it would be bad form to give people the idea that he was a loose cannon. These last few days with Sebastian, however, made all his emotions run hot. Anger was no exception.

The walk back from the admin building did nothing to calm him down. The more he considered the reasoning behind the canceled classes, the worse he felt. Not only did someone decide that his authority wasn't needed to make drastic changes to the upcoming semester, but they'd almost caused Sebastian a bucket-load of anxiety, too. Derek could handle being underestimated, but he was growing more and more protective of Sebastian every day.

He went into the kitchen for a glass of water and to take some time to work out his next move. He pulled out a chair at the kitchen table and sat down. Not twelve hours ago, he and Sebastian had stayed up late talking across this very table. Derek ran his hand over the cool surface. His mind drifted back to last night, how their conversation slowed down, but the looks between them quickened. He tried to remember which one of them had stood up first, but did it matter? The end was the same.

He downed his ice water and sat back, his cheek flushing with the memory of last night. He needed to deal with this situation quickly so he could see Sebastian. He wanted to make sure last night was the start and not the end of something.

A thin hum cut into his thoughts, and he saw a thin black box vibrating at the far end of the table. He reached out, realizing why Sebastian had been ignoring his calls. Turning it over, he saw the missed call screen, but no indication of who made the call. Derek resisted the urge to look further, instantly jealous that Sebastian would have other people he talked to. His little scene in the basement the other day caused a fair bit of damage to a relationship that hadn't even started yet. He stared down at the phone, willing it to ring again. The slab lay silent in his hand. He doubted Sebastian was calling his own phone unless he was trying to locate it.

Realizing that he ought to try Sebastian's office, his own phone buzzed with an email notification. Normally, the college president, even of a small college like Woodlawn, gets inundated with emails every day. Since he'd been dragging his feet hiring an assistant, he was thankful for the second email offered to him for just faculty communication. The idea was that, since Derek's priority should be the running of the school and not outside interests, the faculty and staff should have a direct line to the president so their needs don't get lost in a sea of donor emails. This was the only email he kept on his phone.

Derek glanced at the preview and frowned.

"Derek, I just wanted to get you a list of the classes we

talked about culling next semester. I think it's best to get the catalog for the fall squared away soon, as our incoming students will be setting up their schedules next month. Let's talk about any additions you want to make, and I can help you with the technical details since you're not used to our registration system yet."

Slowly, Derek slid Sebastian's phone into his back pocket, since the urge to toss his phone across the room rose within him. He could imagine the depreciating look on the Dean of Business's face as he wrote the email, thinking himself as the experienced guide of the "boy king." He looked from the kitchen into the study across the hall and saw the framed degree proclaiming Derek's MBA. He felt ashamed.

He moved from the kitchen into the study, imagining how painful it would be to punch a framed degree right in the crest when a knock at the door distracted him.

Derek put on a smile like a jacket and opened the door.

"Seb! Hey, I have your—" As he reached into his back pocket, he felt himself pushed backward into the hall.

"How long?" Sebastian said, holding a painting in between them and using it to push Derek away.

"What?" Derek said, flummoxed.

"How long have you known about your mother and Shaw? Was that the plan all along?"

Derek didn't understand but held out Sebastian's phone anyway, his confused brain thinking that this would solve the problem. It did not.

Sebastian snatched the phone away and pushed the canvas so hard into Derek's chest that he had to take it out of his hands. "What are you doing? What's wrong?"

Sebastian stood in the doorway, breathing heavily but no longer looking straight at Derek. "Did you want to get your hands on the manor easily? Is that why last night—" He stopped, blushing.

Derek opened his mouth but decided against saying anything. He held the canvas away from his chest and looked at it. The large red brick still dominated the left two-thirds of the scene, but now, in the right-hand area near the iron gate, stood a new figure. He leaned closer. No, two new figures.

"Seb, wait, come inside."

"No. I'm done being pulled along by you." He backed out onto the stoop. "You could have just asked. I would have given it to you." Sebastian turned and nearly tripped down onto the front lawn. He stood up and looked back. "You can have everything."

Derek stood there, stunned, unable to move. He looked back down at the painting and at the figure that could be no one other than his mother. That meant the child she was holding could very well be him. He didn't understand what it meant, but more importantly, he didn't understand what Sebastian meant.

Derek raised his head to ask him, but in that moment, Sebastian had disappeared.

38

Sebastian zig-zagged around the small buildings encircling the quad, hoping to keep out of Derek's line of sight. The path back to his office was a straight shot from the president's home's front porch, but he didn't want to be found right now, if at all. The flood of emotions that stirred in his chest when he uncovered the image of Derek and his mother had scared him. Never before did a betrayal feel so personal, so hurtful. In fact, Sebastian wondered as he marched over to Derek's house, when had he ever felt a sense of betrayal before?

The meeting introducing the department cuts? The phone call about his canceled classes? No, both of those felt like bad business, not pain. Neither of those incidents made Sebastian want to run away. He shuffled between two old faculty houses repurposed into administration buildings and caught his breath. He pretended not to be listening out for footsteps.

No, the last time he felt that weird, hurtful betrayal was outside Shaw's office, the night he saw Brian's mother with Shaw, alone.

Sebastian headed toward the parking lot near the art building. He walked slower this time, tears clouding his vision.

He darted out from behind a large azalea bush and slid quickly into his front seat. Hunkering down, Sebastian looked in the rear-view mirror toward the president's house, but he saw no activity out front. He wasn't sure what he'd expected (or hoped for). Derek leading a search party to find him? Perhaps calling in Casey and the whole lacrosse team to scour the campus? He wasn't sure Derek would go to those lengths to find him, and he still wasn't sure whether he wanted to be found.

Sebastian thought that kind of overblown response would be exactly what Derek would do. He'd been pushy since they reunited, never giving Sebastian space to reconcile the Brian he knew as a child with the Derek standing in front of him. He needed time to collapse those years together or time to let Derek fill them with his own story. But Derek didn't want to wait or second-guess any feelings he already had.

Sebastian heard a car door slam, and he slid down further in the driver's seat, cowering like a child. Faint traces of black and green paint lined his palm. He'd quickly wiped away the best of it before he headed to Derek's. He could smell the remnant of thinner he'd used to peel back the layers of paint and time. It's not that he thought Derek knew what the painting was hiding to begin with, but, somewhere connected with years of insecurity and doubt, Sebastian felt that this proved that Shaw was still one step ahead of him.

He laughed to himself at the realization and closed his eyes. Could it be that simple? Could it be that childish? Assuming that Derek/Brian was Shaw's son, how does that change their relationship? They only spent a couple of summers together when they were children. They're not even step-siblings in the legal sense. Sebastian shook his head. It wasn't the realization that Shaw was his biological father. It was the realization that Shaw had more of a claim to Brian than he did.

Rain spotted the window, and the sun dipped behind a band of clouds. He sat up in the seat, steadying his hands on the wheel—ten and two—like Manny had shown him years ago. He looked at his paint-streaked fists. "Derek," he whispered to himself. That's who he was dealing with now—not Brian. They were the same person but separated over time and life experience. The jealousy he felt was the connection to Brian then, not to Derek now.

And, if he were honest to himself, Derek had shown honest shock at his accusation.

He looked at his rear-view and, seeing no last-minute overly romantic pursuit, he started his car and slowly backed out of the small lot. What had he expected? The rain grew steady, and he eased himself onto the main road without looking back. He was going home while he could still call it that.

39

BRIAN, 8 years old

Brian knew he had made a mistake the moment he fell. Mud splashed up all around his small frame and covered his raincoat in dirt and leaves. Finding the path back to the cave had been difficult without Sebastian. He was used to following behind his friend, putting his full trust in his leadership. Now, sitting in the mud alone, he stifled the urge to cry and kept moving forward. He left the manor determined to be the hero of this story. He needed to prove himself to his friend.

He pulled himself up on a small walnut sapling near the trail and shook off as much mud as he could. The rain helped, slick and heavy now, making the already dark night nearly impenetrable, but with each step, he could feel clods of mud squish around his socks. Brian thought he'd probably end up with a summer cold, but he was willing to take the risk.

He ducked under the water-heavy fronds of a large fern, and the cave entrance appeared ahead of him in the gloom. The little amount of moonlight that glowed behind the clouds glistened off the granite outcroppings surrounding the hole. It looked as if the forest had developed a mouth with rock-hard teeth just to swallow up little boys who came along when they should have been asleep in bed. Brian hesitated, watching the water spilling out of the cave entrance. What had been a light trickle when he and Sebastian had been there in the daylight was a vigorous waterfall now. Would he be able to climb up against the strong flow of the water? He'd read in his *National Geographic* how salmon returned home to spawn, sometimes swimming upstream and in some cases swimming directly up waterfalls. He knew he was much bigger than the largest salmon and, by extension, hoped he was stronger. Brian tried hard not to think of the size of the bear that could catch an eight-year-old boy in its jaws.

The hood of his raincoat slipped forward, blinding him as he made his way up the first jutting stones. Steadying himself in the water, he pushed it back up only to have a burst of water splash him in the face. He coughed and grabbed onto a sodden root growing out of the entrance, hoping that it was attached to something tall and sturdy. Water from the sky and from the cave filled the world. He imagined that this is what it sounded like standing near a jet engine, a constant thrumming filling his head. The water smelled of both sky and soil, as if the earth had only briefly separated the two reservoirs until this very night, when this boy wanted to go on an adventure.

Using the root as leverage, he pulled himself to the lip of the cave and sat, catching his breath. The stream pulled around him, tugging at his hips and legs to expel him from the opening. He pulled his knapsack around and unzipped it, hoping at least his flashlight wasn't water-logged. Brian felt the dry metal and relaxed. In his relief, the grip he had on the bag loosened, and the water swept it away.

"No!" He yelled after it, and for some reason, the water

didn't obey. He sat perched on the cusp of going back or going forward, watching his supplies being carried away. He leaned into the cave, holding the flashlight out of the rain, and switched it on. The white beam lit up the rock walls of the cave, and Brian could see a small, mostly dry clearing about ten feet away.

Most of the water was coming in from his right side, a small diversion from a stream he and Sebastian had tried to dam earlier that summer. They nearly had the whole stretch around the cave diverted to make it easier to search until Jim found them. He told them that there was a reason Mother Nature wanted the water to go where it did, and they had no business making changes. Sebastian had argued something about the north end of the stream that diverted into an irrigation ditch for the vegetable gardens, but Jim ushered them back to the house and then snitched to Manny. They'd been prohibited from going to the cave ever since.

Brian swung the flashlight across the interior of the cave. Past the puddle of water sprayed in from the stream, there seemed to be nothing of interest—or at least danger—within the immediate area. He reasoned that if he didn't think he could go further, he could stay in the dry area and wait until the rain stopped. They'd miss him if he didn't come back, and he knew Sebastian would come looking for him.

Deciding to move on, he pulled his leg away from the water and tried to shift his way toward the path of his flashlight. His left hand, still holding the root, slipped, and he lost his balance, plunging face first into the water and tumbling deeper into the cave. Brian rolled, his right hand desperate to keep hold of the flashlight, but his feet bounced off the narrowing walls at the back of the entrance and shifted his body toward the far wall, missing the semi-dry clearing. He slammed into a protrusion of granite and felt his forearm bend at the impact. The force of the water ripped the flashlight out of his hand and pulled it up and back out of the cave. The beam briefly lit up the web of branches just visible from his spot, flickered, and went dark.

Brian soon followed.

WHEN HE WOKE UP, the water had slowed at the cave entrance, but the rain outside sounded muffled, as if it were far away. Brian tried to roll over, but sharp pain shot through his right arm, and he yelled. Tears welled up in his eyes as he lay there, staring up at the rocky ceiling of the cave entrance. He slammed his left hand into the dirt beside him, frustrated. Sebastian would laugh at him. The little kid who followed him around was too weak to even make it inside the cave itself. Why would he take this little, weepy kid on an adventure?

He dug his hand into the ground, the only thing he could move without terrible pain. His fingers found something smooth and cool. Brian sniffled and furrowed his brows, momentarily distracted from his disappointment. He found purchase on the object and slowly coaxed it out of the hard soil. It was flat and circular; he let his fingers feel the shape and circumference of the thing before slowly bringing it up in front of his face. Brian couldn't discern any details through his tears, but he was certain of one thing: The object was definitely a gold coin.

Disallowing any other explanation to enter his mind, Brian clutched the coin in his good hand and tried again to upright himself. Once again, he failed and let out a loud cry that echoed into the farther reaches of the cave. That's when he heard Jim.

"This way, I heard something," he called. Brian tried yelling

Jim's name, but all that came out was a high-pitched humming that ended in a sob.

"Brian," called Manny's voice, lower and more powerful. "Brian, my boy, you down there?"

Brian could hear the men shouting to each other about getting rope and the mini tractor. He called up again, this time belting out a clear "I'm here!" He looked down at the coin in his left hand, and butterflies filled his stomach. He could show Sebastian what he found, and maybe that would be enough to stay by his side.

"I'm here," he called again, stronger this time, and instead of trying to sit up, he stashed the coin into the pocket of his jeans and waited.

He heard Manny tell him to sit tight. He heard Jimmy yell that the rope was ready. He heard the two men scrabbling for a foothold at the entrance. When he saw the friendly face of Manny appear in the cave opening like a sunrise, Brian started crying again. He cried harder and deeper, nearly hyperventilating, when the groundskeeper finally knelt next to his broken body.

"S'ok, my boy, let's get you out of here. Be still."

Brian nodded through his whimpering and let himself be carried up to the entrance. Manny gently handed the boy to Jim. He could see the thick rope around each man's waist. They were tethered to each other, with Jimmy tethered to a large oak on the other side of the trail. In that moment, Brian realized how Manny and Jimmy were friends, how they relied on each other, and how they were completely connected. To Brian, they were real friends and real heroes.

· · ·

As Jimmy put him in the back of the small tractor, Brian turned his head from side to side. Sunlight cleared most of the gloom of the forest from the night before, and he could see the far end of the trail he followed to the cave. Had it always been this close to the gardens?

Manny exited the cave and went straight toward Jim, giving him a hard clap on the shoulder. "Well done," he said. "Let's get him back."

Brian felt that clap in the pit of his stomach, scaring off the butterflies and the excitement. He turned his head again, desperate to find his friend waiting for him, but Sebastian was nowhere to be found.

"Kid's really hurting," Jimmy said sympathetically as Brian wailed.

40

DEREK PARKED HAPHAZARDLY behind Sebastian's car on the gravel driveway. As he approached the door, he realized he hadn't been back at the manor in almost 15 years, but as he neared the brick facade, he noticed that not much had changed. He paused on the stoop before the mahogany door and rehearsed in his mind what would happen. He imagined Sebastian opening the door and trying to slam it in his face again. Derek wondered if he should grab the door and force himself inside or just wait patiently out front until Sebastian had to talk to him. He didn't rehearse what he was going to say because he had no idea what to say.

It's not that the revelation was preposterous—it was something his mother had always hinted at when he was young. It's that he never thought that Shaw being his biological father—if true—mattered. He didn't want anything from Shaw, and his mother certainly had never sought anything but love, which was never returned. To Brian, this had never been Shaw Manor, but Sebastian's home. For Derek, it remained the same, and without Sebastian, the place held no meaning.

He took a deep breath and raised his hand just as the door opened. Beverly, older but still possessing the kind and hearty face he remembered, stood there. She raised an eyebrow and frowned. "Do we know you?"

"Beverly! It's me. Brian." Derek pointed at himself as if to emphasize it was him.

Her eyes narrowed, and she stepped onto the lip of the door frame. She tapped the inside wall near the lock and pulled the door shut behind her.

"I see," she said. "What does Mr. President want with Shaw Manor today?" Beverly folded her arms and waited.

The smile dimmed on Derek's face as he received the cold welcome. He heard heavy footsteps on the gravel to his right. He caught movement in his periphery and turned in time to see an older, grayer Manny step onto the driveway through the iron gate. It swung shut with a metallic squeal. Derek's heart skipped a beat, thinking of the image of him and his mother painted in that very spot. Damn Campbell Shaw. The old man is still coming between them.

"Hi Manny. How are you? Do—"

"I know who you are, my boy." The groundskeeper stopped and put his hands into the front pockets of his overalls. "I know who you are." He didn't follow up with a question.

Derek understood he was being delayed. "Where's Sebastian?" he asked, dropping the niceties.

"Sebastian's not in the house," Beverly said. "I can tell him you came by."

Derek said nothing, but turned to Manny, then Beverly, then to the blue bulk of Sebastian's car in the driveway. He hadn't expected to run into these blasts from the past, certainly not in this situation. All his imagination had been of the romantic variety, big gestures guaranteed to win over Sebastian even at his most obstinate. He knew that if he couldn't win him over in argument, he had enough charm to at least prolong the conversation until he wore him down. Derek had spent too many years away from Sebastian to let these two stop him now. But Brian's memories of Beverly and Manny's kindness muddied the situation.

"I just want to explain—"

"Why not call tomorrow morning and ask him to come to you?" Beverly said.

Derek stared at her, knowing she had full authority to send him away but determined not to leave until he saw Sebastian. He heard Manny take a few steps toward him, the sound of crunching gravel emphasizing the threat.

Dammit, he thought, and stepped backwards off the stoop. Beverly smiled. He saw Manny relax his shoulders, and Derek made his move. He took off at a run, sidestepping Manny's outstretched arm, and wrenched open the metal gate. Thankfully, Manny forgot to lock it behind him. Probably thought I'd cave, he thought, running easily along the round pavers, missing none, and avoiding the spaces in between. He smiled as he felt his body recognizing the gardens on the side of the building.

He heard Manny calling after him, and he quickened his pace. He couldn't have the big gesture at the front of the house, he thought, but there was only one place that Sebastian could be hiding. His body easily turned towards the meadow and the edge of the forest. The voices behind him faded away, and, for the first time since he was a child, he ran, laughing all the way.

41

DEREK SPOTTED him before he reached the old oak tree. He stood in the middle of the trail, hoping to be noticed, but Sebastian sat staring at the ground around the cave entrance. There had been little rain that spring, and the water coming out of the cave was barely a trickle. He took a step forward and stopped again, the sound of water rushing through a narrowing space filled his head. Goosebumps broke out along his shoulders and his right forearm ached. He'd never returned to Shaw Manor after being carried out of the cave. It was if that instance had shifted him into a new timeline, one where Sebastian had been an imaginary friend.

He slowly moved closer, watching the breeze lift up the curls of Sebastian's dark hair. Derek felt he saw two versions of his friend, sitting on the granite outcropping and wondered whether it was he or Brian that approached.

"I don't know where you got that coin," Sebastian said, not looking up. "But there's never been any treasure here."

Derek stopped at the base of the cave entrance only a few feet from where Sebastian sat, but didn't say anything. He didn't even know where to start. He knew where the coin came from. He could still feel it on his fingers. He remembered how he dug it out of the ground. Bringing up the coin startled him, and he didn't know how to continue. He decided to take a different approach.

"All I know is that my treasure has always been here." His heartbeat rang in his ears and he felt the flush rise from his neck to his cheeks. He waited, watching.

Turning toward Derek, Sebastian scowled. He pulled his hand out of his right pocket and extended his middle finger. "What the hell?"

Sebastian slipped off the small ledge above the cave entrance and walked toward him. Derek stepped back, readying for a punch or a lecture. It didn't matter which, at least he was talking to him.

As Sebastian approached, he only sighed.

"Did you look at the painting?" He asked.

"Yeah."

"That's definitely you and your mother."

"Yeah. I think so, too." Derek kept his replies short, giving Sebastian all the time he needed.

"You know what that means?"

Derek tilted his head. "That Shaw painted us outside the manor when I was an infant."

Sebastian frowned. "What were you doing here as a baby if you're not Shaw's—"

"What does it matter?" Derek interrupted, unable to hold back any longer. On the drive over, he thought about Campbell Shaw and what being his son would mean. He felt nothing about Shaw. The man had been some shadowy figure in the background, someone his mother fawned over. By the end of that first summer, world famous Campbell Shaw had been a means to an end for Brian—that end being Sebastian. He didn't care about anything else.

Yet, he understood that Sebastian had a different, more significant relationship with the man. He could sense there were a lot of insecurities there, baggage he wanted to help him unpack. He could feel the presence of the house behind him, sitting like a brick slab at the edge of their forest. Yes, he thought, *our* forest. He took in somewhat taller trees and the overgrown ferns. This is ours, no matter what.

"Why does anything about that stupid house matter?" Derek asked.

Sebastian looked away. "It matters if it's yours. It matters because all this time, you—"

"I was what? His son? His heir? Are you worried about being kicked out if I claim ownership? Is that all you care about is property rights?"

He stomped past Sebastian and peered into the cave entrance. It seemed so much smaller than his memory. Now, he could easily bend down and see the clearing where he'd fallen. The sunlight illuminated just enough to bring his memories flooding back, but this time, fear didn't come with them. Derek turned back to Sebastian, angry.

"As far as I'm concerned, you and I could crawl into the stupid cave and live there. Shaw is nothing to me. This house and this land are nothing to me without you here. What don't you get?"

Sebastian lifted his head, but didn't reply.

"You think you've uncovered some conspiracy? You think I seduced you to get your damn house?" He kicked at a pile of stone on the ground. His frustration increased, and once again he could feel that coin under his fingers. The coin Sebastian had just said couldn't exist.

"Derek, look—"

"Shut up," Derek spat. "You think I stayed away because I was biding my time? I didn't know you were here. I didn't come look for you because I didn't think you'd want to be found." He raised his voice, unable to stop himself, and pointed to the cave entrance behind him.

"Where were you when I was in there? When they brought me out, you were nowhere to be found." He could feel tears running down his cheeks. His heart raced, but he plowed forward.

"I worshiped you. I wanted to be with you forever. But you didn't come looking for me. You didn't come looking for me, *ever*."

Sebastian stood wide-eyed and took a step forward. Derek held out his hand to stop him.

"You should have been there. I was so," his voice faltered. "I was so scared, Seb. I was so, so scared."

Sebastian grabbed Derek's shoulders and pulled him into a hug. Derek pulled away at first but then let himself be held. He buried his face in Sebastian's neck and sobbed. "I was so scared," he repeated. He grabbed the back of Sebastian's shirt and held on. He wasn't going to lose him again.

He'd never be scared again.

SEBASTIAN HELD ON, letting Derek calm down and back away on his own. He'd never experienced such anger directed at him before and had to admit that he'd spent his life keeping himself distant enough from people that no one cared enough to yell at him. Shaw mostly treated him like a project or pupil. Only the occasional lectures from Beverly and Manny helped Sebastian avoid turning into a complete ass.

As Derek backed away, he grabbed Sebastian's hands, as if holding on for dear life. For a moment, he looked like a taller version of Brian standing there, looking hopeful and scared at the same time. He thought about how the little blond kid would follow him around and his heart felt heavy in his chest. Brian had made him feel important, but he never once thought about how he made Brian feel. He looked up into Derek's swollen face and tried to understand.

"They kept me back from the cave," Sebastian explained. "I saw Jimmy go inside and that was it. Shaw grabbed me from behind and took me back to the house." He could still feel the strong arms hoisting him into the air, but that was all.

Thinking back, Shaw must have been worried that it would be too traumatic if Brian were badly hurt.

"I think he was trying to protect me, but I fought him," Sebastian said. "I kicked and yelled. Beverly told me later that I actually bit him. I don't remember much after that." He tightened his grip on the hands holding his. Derek leaned forward and put his head back on Sebastian's shoulder.

"Shaw and I were never really close after that. Your mom blamed me. She made it seem like you were dead, but Manny explained. I think Shaw must have blamed himself for a long time." Sebastian leaned his forehead on Derek's. "When you never came back, then I thought it was my fault. I should never have shown you this place. I never should have made you think we could explore it."

Derek chuckled and raised his head. "I'll never forget the look on your face when you talked about looking for treasure in that cave. That's probably the moment I fell for you."

Sebastian blushed and his whole body felt as if electricity ran through his veins.

Derek whispered something close to his ear, but he didn't understand. "What?"

"Why didn't you look for me?"

Sebastian pushed Derek back but still held onto his hands. He wanted to look directly at him. "How could I? My parents' accident was soon after you left and then I was suddenly having to live up to this." He gestured at the grounds and the manor and the sky.

"All of a sudden I was some legacy of the great Campbell Shaw. It wasn't something I ever wanted.

"It took a long time just to find myself, and to be honest, I'm still half lost." He leaned closer to Derek to make his point again. "You weren't exactly looking for me, either."

Derek nodded and looked guilty, and Sebastian's heart warmed at the expression. For too long they'd been separated by circumstances, stupidity, and, if he was honest, ego. Clouds rolled in and the light reaching the forest floor dimmed. Sebastian shivered, whether from the cooling breeze or the warmth in Derek's eyes, he wasn't sure.

"I think we are both a couple of idiots," Sebastian said. Derek looked at him, eyebrows raised, but didn't disagree.

Light ran pattered on the canopy above as they kissed. Derek wrapped his arms around Sebastian's waist and pulled him closer. Sebastian pulled away at the distant roll of thunder.

"Let's get inside," he said. "You still hate thunderstorms, don't you?"

43

SEBASTIAN SLID against the far wall of the kitchen until he was in front of Beverly's office door. He smiled at the throng of people milling about fixing hor'doeuvres, pouring wine, and partaking in the delicate culinary art of the academic get-together. He reached behind his back and tried the doorknob. Locked. Should have known. Beverly always worried that the caterers would nose about her business while they took over her kitchen, so she made sure to keep them far from her special papers.

From across the kitchen, he heard a lilting laugh and was surprised it was coming from Beverly herself.

She stood next to a tall, handsome man in his mid-forties, whom Sebastian took for the caterer. Never before had he seen Beverly speak so happily to someone infiltrating her kitchen, but to Sebastian's inexperienced eye, he suspected that this was her way of flirting. He grunted and quickly imagined a future where Beverly went off with a handsome chef and left him alone to make his own dinner.

He felt a presence next to him, and the scent of soil and

mint filled his nostrils. "You know you're more than welcome to join the party," Sebastian said.

Manny stood next to him, pressed against the wall. "Nah, my boy. Too fancy for the likes of me. Besides…" Sebastian noticed he was keeping a close eye on Beverly from across the room. His kind face showed traces of distrust and worry. "I'd like to keep an eye on Beverly. Make sure no weirdos are bothering her."

Sebastian looked from Manny to the handsome weirdo in question and smiled.

He caught sight of a new entrant into the room. Wait staff and assistants passed back and forth in the space between them and the rest of the kitchen and completely blocked the approach of the guest of honor.

"If you're hiding in here, so am I," Derek said, parking himself on the other side of Sebastian. He leaned forward and gave Manny a little wave. The groundskeeper nodded in return but said nothing. Over the past week, the two had formed an uneasy truce, but Sebastian could tell that Manny was still smarting from being outmaneuvered by Derek. Sebastian felt that Derek being little Brian all grown up made the whole thing even harder for Manny to take.

The three men stood against the wall like cardboard cutouts of an old comedy trio. Thankfully, no one in the catering staff gave them much notice. The looks on their faces, particularly Manny's jealous scowl, could have spoiled even the most carefully crafted canapes.

Sebastian elbowed Derek. "You're the main attraction here. You should be out there hobnobbing with donors."

Derek slouched. "I've been doing that all week. I don't need to hear the same old stories over and over again. Some of them have decided their best days were at Woodlawn."

"What's wrong with that? That devotion's good for the school, right?"

Derek nodded. "But it's not good for my sanity. I've got enough pulling me away from spending time with you as it is."

Sebastian blushed and slid his hand into Derek's. "When's the committee hearing?"

"Tuesday. The Dean of Business is not expected to offer up any explanation. He admitted to using my credentials to alter registration, and that's that."

"What did I ever do to that guy?"

Derek shrugged. "No idea. You know he showed up here, right?"

Sebastian turned to him. "What?"

Manny muttered something about caterers and slid out the small door that opens onto the garden.

"Jim escorted him off the property. It was comedy gold." Derek laughed and seemed to relax. Sebastian turned back to the hustle and bustle of the kitchen and wondered if he and Derek could just stay there together, forever unnoticed, unbothered, and side-by-side.

Two young men in wait staff uniforms approached, each carrying a tray of tiny desserts.

"Hey, Dr. Tate. What are you doing over here?" Casey strode up and turned his tray like a professional, presenting Sebastian with a selection of tarts. He glanced once at Derek, then back to Sebastian. He winked. "Want a taste?"

Sebastian wrinkled up his face at the joke and reached for a dessert. He could feel Derek move closer to him and felt the atmosphere turn cold. He popped the tiny tart into his mouth. He looked from Casey to his friend and back again. The black vests and long aprons suited them. An elbow in his side made him turn.

Derek stared at him. "Don't take sweets from strangers."

Sebastian swallowed. "Casey's not a stranger."

"Pretty strange to me," Derek said, watching the two saunter out of the kitchen with their trays.

Before Sebastian could reply, Beverly appeared, flushed and a bit tipsy. She'd broken away from her handsome chef and discovered the two of them cowering near her office. Her smile turned to cold disappointment as she leaned into her two young charges.

"You two," she said, bringing a finger up to stick in their faces. "You two need to get out of my kitchen. I don't care where you go, but you're not to hide in here."

Sebastian and Derek accepted the scolding and slid away toward the door Manny had just used. The welcome party of the new president of Woodlawn College seemed to be going just fine without its host and guest of honor, and they saw no reason to return. They slipped out the door, Sebastian pulling Derek by the hand, and spent the rest of the day outside, looking for adventure.

ABOUT THE AUTHOR

Hartlee Finn lives in the Mid-Atlantic area of the United States and has the accent to prove it. While not writing about idiots in love, she thinks about how she *should be writing* while playing Stardew Valley and helping students write their college essays.

For more information about Hartlee and to get updates on the next book in the Woodlawn College Series, sign up for her newsletter at hartleefinn.com

WHAT ABOUT CASEY?

Casey Stanfield passed through *Art History* like an athletic cupid, dropping hints and winks everywhere.

The star of the Wildcats lacrosse team has his own troubles and love story coming up next in *Lacrossed Lovers: A Woodlawn College Romance.*

Lacrossed Lovers is available now!

ALSO BY HARTLEE FINN

The Woodlawn College Romance Series

Art History

Lacrossed Lovers

Book 3 coming soon!